★★★★★ Wh...

Wow, what a phe...
simple and light-h...
completely unexpected plot twists, and just when it seems like there's a bunch of loose ends... Bam! They all come together in a massive, rock-your-world sort of ending that, strangely enough, makes complete sense. It's clean fun in a fast-paced fantasy action setting from start to finish. Definitely one of my favorites. This guy has some serious talent. I look forward to the next season!
- Author Joel Babbit

★★★★★ **A wonderful and unusual, fantasy adventure**

A non-stop, tongue-in-cheek fantasy adventure that was both highly entertaining while at the same time, admittedly, frankly absurd.
But the strongest asset of this book, was not the story itself (and it was very good), but rather the truly wondrous characters the populated its pages and brought this unusual tale to life.
So relax, find a comfortable chair, have some snacks handy and be prepared to be entertained by this preposterous, yet wonderfully written and engaging tale.
- R Nicholson, an Amazon Reviewer

★★★★★ **A Fantasy Book for Serious Fantasy Readers**

A very fast-paced, fun read with a great cast of very likable characters. I loved it.
- Nathan, an Amazon Reviewer

THE BERSERKER AND THE PEDANT

JOSH POWELL

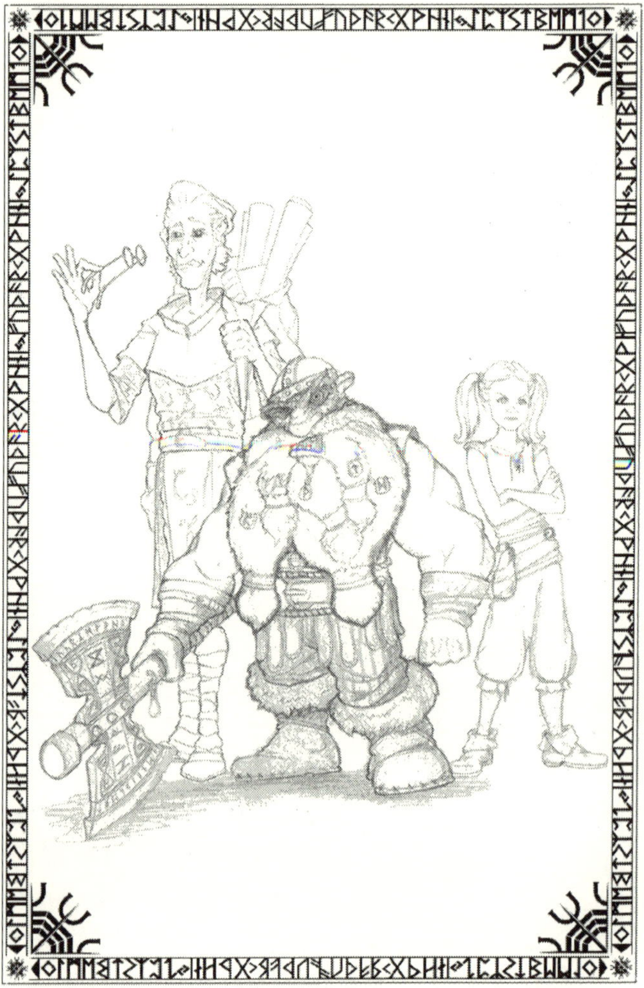

This book is dedicated to
Liam and Chloe

My berserker and little girl

This is a work of fiction. All of the characters, organizations, and events portrayed in this novel are either products of the author's imagination or are used fictitiously.

THE BERSERKER AND THE PEDANT

Copyright © 2015 by Josh Powell

Editor: Marta Tanrikulu

Cover Art: James E. Grant

Interior Art: Milan C.

All rights reserved.

340 S Lemon Ave #4745
Walnut Ca 91789
USA

Reproduction in whole or part of this publication without express written consent is strictly prohibited. Thank you for reading, I really appreciate you choosing to spend your valuable time reading my work. Please think about leaving a review for THE BERSERKER AND THE PEDANT wherever you purchased the book, or tell your friends about it, and then drop me a line. Leaving a review will help me out more than anything else you can do. If you do leave a review, let me know and I'll either send you Season Two for free when it comes out or add you to my beta readers (whichever your prefer).

Contents

Pilot	The Berserker and the Pedant	13
Episode 1	The Berserker and the Sweet Cake	21
Episode 2	The Berserker and the Sleep Sack	30
Episode 3	The Berserker and the Ant	38
Episode 4	The Berserker and the Minotaur	46
Episode 5	The Berserker and the Centaur	55
Episode 6	The Berserker and the Patrol	65
Episode 7	The Berserker and the Elf	73
Episode 8	The Berserker and the Trolls	82
Episode 9	The Berserker and the Goblins	91
Episode 10	The Berserker and the Pedants	99
Episode 11	The Berserker and the Rescue	108
Episode 12	The Berserker and the Awakening	116
Episode 13	The Berserker and the Orb	125
Episode 14	The Berserker and the Cave	134
Episode 15	The Berserker and the Walnut	143
Episode 16	The Berserker and the Elves	151
Episode 17	The Berserker and the Pedant	161
	Epilogue	170
	Afterword	180
	About the Author	183

Introduction

The *Berserker and the Pedant* is an epic fantasy adventure filled with humor, twists and turns, and some very lovable characters. You'll laugh out loud, you'll cry, and you'll shout "How ridiculous!" only to chuckle and keep on reading.

When you're left wanting more, meander over to http://www.pedantpublishing.com and subscribe to the mailing list, you'll immediately receive a short story that reveals some of the hidden secrets of the world, and is guaranteed to make you laugh.

If you enjoy *The Berserker and the Pedant,* please leave a review. No, really. I need reviews. No reviews, no sales. No sales, no more books. Okay, fine, there will be more books because I love writing them. Please leave a review anyway.

Thank you for reading. Let me know if you liked the book, contact me @seasoup on Twitter.

Acknowledgements

My biggest thanks to my wife, Marianne. Without her help I would never have had time to write a book. She also acted as a sounding board for discussing ideas, and as my first reader, and my best cheerleader.

Special thanks to Ray Nicholson for doing a beta read and providing quality feedback before the book was finished. In particular, his guidance shaped the description of the word "pedant" in the first chapter, solving an ongoing issue readers were having.

Pilot

The Berserker and the Pedant

⚔

Gurken Stonebiter gulped for air as he ran in hot pursuit of a temple thief. He was not about to stop before he apprehended the miscreant. The thief hurdled a barrel, slid through the legs of a horse, and leapt into a building, slamming the door. Gurken Stonebiter, dwarven templerager, and avatar of the great dwarven god of butchery and battle, Durstin Firebeard, was thwarted.

Gurken thought about hacking down the door, and nearly did - nearly, but for the thought that breaking through such a thick door would cause a certain dullness to accumulate on the blade. Not wanting to endure the drudgery of honing his axe, Gurken sprinted around the building looking for another entrance. Finding none, he returned to stand watch at the door, axe ready to strike, waiting for the thief to exit.

Some time later, a small girl wandered up to Gurken. She raised an eyebrow and smiled at him.

Gurken was a towering figure - for a dwarf, as such, he was barely taller than the young girl. Built

THE BERSERKER AND THE PEDANT

like a rhinoceros, his muscles rippled over his body. His neck was solid as a granite statue. Despite his great height, he was overly wide due first to his massive torso and second to his chainmail armor and layers of padding. He wore a dented metal cap covering his bald head. His earthy red beard was caked with an ornamental red clay, and the many small scars on his face displayed his affection for combat. He looked quite formidable, unapproachable, and capable of unnerving even the bravest of soldiers.

"What are you doing?" the girl inquired. If she was unnerved in any way, she hid it quite well.

Gurken lowered his head and peered at the girl. "I await the thief within this building, boy."

"I'm not a boy! I'm a girl. Why don't you go inside?"

Gurken's brow furled. "Look here, boy..."

"I'm not a-" she interrupted.

"Never interrupt a berserker, boy," said Gurken, lowering his axe, "I'm Gurken Stonebiter and I'm about the business of the temple of Durstin Firebeard. I'm pursuing the vilest kind of villain - a thief that has stolen temple property. He fled into this building, and so I'm waiting for him to come out in order to make an arrest. If I must, I shall wait until..."

She hadn't intended to interrupt again, but it seemed as if Gurken was going to continue for quite some time.

"Pleasure to meet you, Gurken, I'm Pellonia. Why don't you go inside?"

Gurken almost noticed that she interrupted him again, but missed it because of the abrupt change in topic. "I was just getting to that. Ordinarily, I would go inside and apprehend the criminal, but just now, I am stymied."

"Stymied, you say?"

"Yes, stymied," he agreed, nodding.

"Thwarted even?"

"Why, yes, that is just so. I'm thwarted," said Gurken, pleased with the unusual feeling of being understood.

"I can see why being thwarted would stop you from going inside. But, that begs the question, what's thwarting you?"

"A fair question, boy." It had been some time since anyone had taken such an active interest in him.

She sighed. "I had thought it fair."

"And it was, I insist on it." Gurken thought that he should be pleasant in return.

"Well, please answer, what thwarts you from going inside?"

"Ah. That. Well, it is locked. I have no key, nor wish to dull my axe which would require some amount of time sharpening to restore its keen edge. So I wait."

THE BERSERKER AND THE PEDANT

"Well, I have an answer for you. Watch this."

She turned the knob, and the door opened. Gurken was astonished!

"You're a master lock pick!"

"A what? Master loc - no I'm not." She raised her hands defensively in front of her.

"Come to think of it, a master of locks is also a master of disguise," he said. The feeling of understanding gave way to that of betrayal, having been deceived by a promising new friend.

"Um, what? No, no no. It wasn't locked."

Gurken, though having many admirable qualities, seemed unable or unwilling to hear something contrary to the way he thought things were.

"You almost fooled me, master thief, but you weren't quite good enough to fool Gurken Stonebiter! You should surrender now, for you won't like what I will have to do if I were forced to apprehend you."

"I'm not a thief! I'm a little girl!"

"Please come this way, or you shall make me wroth. You won't like it when I'm wroth, for there is much bloodshed, butchery, and death." He paused a moment, putting a finger on his lip, then continued, "and not my death, I assure you. Other persons's deaths." A small crowd had gathered, watching the interaction between the unusual looking dwarf and the small girl. The crowd began to look a bit nervous.

"My death?" She gulped.

"Other people's." He shrugged. "Perhaps yours. You see I tend not to be particular."

Her eyes widened and she put her hands up. "I surrender!" She didn't seem to want the death of others on her conscience.

"Pardon me sir," came a voice from behind. "If I might interject."

Gurken turned and looked into the midriff of a stranger, dressed in a fine sapphire blue silken robe, embroidered with numerous symbols along the hem. He smelled of books and ink. This was not going to go well.

Gurken shook his head from side to side, then he casually inclined his head to look up at the man.

"You sir, are interjecting my arrest."

The man wrinkled his brow. "Perhaps I'm being a pedant, but..."

"I'm sorry," said Gurken. "But, did you call yourself a pendant?"

"A pedant - one who may, on occasion, have a tendency to overemphasize the rules of grammar and/or logic, that is, to be pedantic."

Gurken just glared at him.

"As I was saying, perhaps I'm being a pedant, but you didn't use the word 'interjecting' properly. However, I understand your meaning, and you are correct, I am interrupting you, but with good reason.

THE BERSERKER AND THE PEDANT

You see, that girl is not guilty of the crime of which you accuse her. My name is Arthur Gimble. I'm a wizard of the tenth rank. I've been practicing the art of perception for a decade, so I'm well equipped to perceive your mistake."

Gurken's eyebrows furrowed. He was perturbed, though not yet wroth.

"Pendant wizard, I'm Gurken Stonebiter, of the dwarfen clan Stonebiter..."

"Dwarven," said Arthur Gimble, sighing. "It's 'dwarven' clan."

Though Gurken was practically unable or unwilling to hear things that conflicted with his viewpoint, Arthur Gimble managed to wedge a toe in the door to comprehension.

"What exactly do you mean?"

"The proper grammatical structure when using 'dwarf' as a proper descriptive adjective is to use the word 'dwarven'. Not 'dwarfen'."

Upon hearing this, Gurken's face flushed with heat, a ringing echoed in his ears, the hair on the back of his neck stood erect, and his eyes engorged with blood, imparting a crimson haze to the world. Hagalaz, the dwarfen rune of catastrophe and short-term disappointment, glowed scarlet on the head of his axe.

Gurken snarled, "I'm afraid I don't understand. Won't you please spell it out for me?"

Arthur spoke obliviously, quite obliviously, with

the regrettable ignorance of one having never been in a fight and unable to sense one approaching. Arthur Gimble, wizard of the tenth rank, took the dwarf quite literally and said, "Dwarven. D. W. A. R. V. Hgurk!"

This last sound was not the wizard explaining how to spell 'dwarven', so much as a reaction to the axe, implanted between his toes and foot.

"Hgaaack!" Being a wizard, one can only imagine that Arthur's first response to being assaulted would be the casting of a devastating spell, meant to cripple, maim, or at least render his foe incapacitated. Arthur found casting a spell, however, to be quite difficult with the flat of an axe slamming into the bottom of his chin, shattering his teeth, mandible, and the rest of his head below the nose.

"Hmmmph." One can hardly blame poor Arthur for continuing to fail to unleash dreaded wizarding power, what with the butt of an axe shoving the wind out of him by being rudely thrust into his gut.

"Roooaaarggghhh!" This was not a sound uttered by the wizard, but let us not think poorly of him for this. He found himself unable to speak, as he was somewhat hindered by the axe etching a deep red gash from his right shoulder through his left hip. No, this was the sound Gurken made as he plunged into his full berserker fury.

If you've never borne witness to a dwarve...

THE BERSERKER AND THE PEDANT

dwarfen templerager in the midst of a berserk fury... well, of course you haven't, you're reading this. They strike with complete abandon, making no attempt to defend while they hack and hew through friend and foe alike. They don't feel any pain, nor suffer from anything like judgment, morality, or sense of propriety until they calm down.

When people tell of the carnage found the next day, they don't speak of a small dwarf and his young prisoner, but of a savage demon. No mortal could have left behind such a slaughter; so many hacked off limbs, disemboweled corpses, and decapitated bodies. The lone known survivor was a wizard of the tenth rank. He could hardly utter a coherent thought except "blood... pain... blood... so much... death. It's dwarfen, dear gods... mercy... it's dwarfen."

And he died.

Hours later, but before anyone had come to move the bodies, the little girl walked up to the gruesome scene. Alone. After a brief survey of the carnage, she walked over to Arthur's body.

"Well, Arthur," said the little girl, looking wistfully into her coin pouch. "Having you mended is going to be costly."

Episode One

THE BERSERKER AND THE SWEET CAKE

🪓

"Most likely, I'll find you dead in the morning," Gurken Stonebiter grinned at the thought. He spoke with the deep grumbling of a dwarf lost in pleasant thought. "Bones picked clean by the rats and small bitey insects."

"Like ants?" asked Pellonia, smiling with the easy charm of a young girl.

"Yes," Gurken replied, glowering at her. "Now be quiet. If you in somehow manage to cheat death, we'll set off for the Mines of Moog at first light. If you insist upon trying to escape, I shall become wroth. Remember, I've got an axe." He held his axe in one hand and pointed at it with the other, scowling.

Pellonia couldn't help but smile. Gurken stowed the axe on his back, clamped shut the irons on her leg and stomped out of the dungeon in a huff.

"I think I like him," Pellonia said. She was tall for a girl of twelve, though one wouldn't know it because she was sitting on the floor.

"He's hardly the sympathetic sort," Arthur

THE BERSERKER AND THE PEDANT

sniffed.

"You don't like him?"

"I tend not to like people that kill me. Mind you, I didn't know that until today, seeing as today was my first experience with dying and returning to life. I believe the priests called it resurrection. I didn't enjoy the experience and hope I never need to repeat it. No, I don't like him."

"You do hold a grudge."

Arthur's mouth hung open.

"Well, Arthur," she said, changing the subject. "It's a fine bit of trouble you've gotten us into." She yanked on the chain to see if she could pull it from the wall.

"Me? I was dead! You're the one that chose to go back to the temple of Durstin." Arthur reconsidered his logic. "Thank you for that, by the way. I'm very much obliged."

"It's Dwarven, not Dwarfen," Pellonia sing songed in her best Arthur Gimble, wizard of the tenth rank impression. It wasn't very good but what it lacked in accuracy it made up for in bass and mockery. "D. W. A. R. Hgurk!" She struck at her head with one hand, as if swinging an axe, then put both of her hands around her neck, pretending to choke herself, and fell over, legs jutting up in the air. She twitched a few times for effect.

"Yes. Well. Fine, quite right then," Arthur somehow managed to look dignified, even though he was suspended upside down against the wall, manacles hanging him up by his ankles.

"A geas," Pellonia said, changing the subject yet again. She climbed to her feet and fiddled with the manacles. "I can't believe they placed us under a geas.

"Under a what?" Arthur asked, looking up but seeing no sign of water fowl.

"A geese," Pellonia continued. "It just doesn't seem right. Why 'mystically compel' us to complete their dumb quest? I returned their stupid holy artifact." Pellonia grumbled, "It's not fair, they just assumed we stole it."

"Ah, it's pronounced geas. And you did steal it," said Arthur, waving a hand towards her. "Hence, geas. Why did you return it, anyway?"

She muttered under her breath.

"Pardon?" said Arthur, "but I couldn't hear you."

"I saaaiiid, 'They said they needed it to mend you. They said couldn't mend anyone without it.'"

"I'm really quite flabbergasted; that's rather companionable of you."

"Stuff it, Arthur."

Gurken arrived the next morning, humming a light-hearted dwarfen tune. He walked up to the dungeon; it was a small building hewn from large rocks, and had a rather rough finish. Inside was but

THE BERSERKER AND THE PEDANT

the one room, which at various times held gardening tools, mundane temple supplies such as paper and spare vestments, or, as it does presently, prisoners. It was the contents, then, not the configuration of the structure that determined its classification. And so, the building was, in turn, a gardening shed, a storage room, and, just now, a dungeon.

Gurken left his chainmail armor behind, in favor of a somewhat less cumbersome, though to be sure, more uncomfortable and prone to chaff, oiled leather armor he favored for travel. He still wore his dented metal cap and his beard was still caked with an earthy red clay. He carried a traveling pack, within which were heavily salted fish, a shovel, and three sleep sacks. The shopkeeper from which he had purchased the sleep sacks had assured him that they would provide his questing party some layer of protection from rain, uncomfortable rocks, and insects which had a propensity to bite in places that one ought not be bit.

Gurken walked towards the dungeon's entrance and, rather pleased at the prospect of adventure, began to narrate the start of the quest. He had practiced many times since the priests of Durstin told him take the treacherous temple thieves and fetch the Orb of Seeza... The Orb of Sizank... Such and such, doesn't matter. The point was it had fallen into the hands of evildoers and that the three of them were to reclaim the orb.

"Well then, fellow travelers. As you can see, or at least you will once we've stepped beyond the confines of this dungeon. The sun has begun to peek over the distant horizon, the birds shall soon be chirping, and there is a fine, crisp chill in the air. It's time to be off." Gurken was rather proud, this being more words than he often bothered to string together. So he was rather dismayed to find he lacked a proper audience; the dungeon was empty (if one can call an empty room a dungeon).

On the floor were the chains with which he had bound the little thief. The manacles were open, lacking the former prisoner. And there on the wall were the fetters he used to bind Arthur, though one would be forgiven for confusing the fetters with the type of wall ornamentation used to organize various shovels, rakes, and other tools of considerable length that one used in the course of gardening. Seeing that there were not prisoners in this dungeon, Gurken left the way he had come.

Standing in front of the dungeon (or, perhaps, the gardening shed), Gurken began to think. His mind set off in the direction of arriving at the opinion that Arthur and Pellonia had escaped. This laborious task was cut short in the nick of time.

"I say there," Arthur interjected, "Gurken, good fellow! It's good to see you, let us be off, for the birds have begun to sing, and if you look yonder, you'll see the sun beginning to peek over the distant horizon."

THE BERSERKER AND THE PEDANT

Arthur and Pellonia walked up to the gardening shed, crumbs from sweet cake about their attire, holding mugs of freshly brewed coffee, and stopped in front of Gurken.

"I see that you are no longer bound," Gurken said, frowning, an expression to which he was most accustomed, "I begin to suspect that you've attempted an escape."

"Escape? Come now, that's an interesting word," said Arthur, nervously gulping down the last mouthful of his sweet cake, beads of sweat forming on his brow. He tugged on the collar of his robe, as if to relieve heat and pressure building up from within.

"Far from interesting," Gurken said, "I think it a most mundane word. A word so mundane, in fact, as to be deserving of an axe!" Gurken swung the axe off his back with his right hand and thrust it into the air in one expert motion. Ansuz, the dwarfen rune of insight and communication glowed bright orange and upside down on the head of the axe, the low hum of a flawless tuning fork vibrating Arthur's teeth and soul. Gurken's face went flush, "or even, perhaps, a shovel!" He pulled the shovel off his pack with his left hand, thrusting it towards Arthur. A few flecks of mud flicked off, splutting on Arthur's face.

Arthur said something to the effect of "Oh no, not again." His words sounded far off to Gurken, as if spoken from the other end of a large chamber and echoing several times in order to arrive at his ears.

Everything seemed to stretch and pull away and dim.

"Gurken," said Pellonia, hardly seeming to notice, "if we were trying to escape, would we have brought you coffee and sweet cake?"

Gurken was surprised at this statement. So surprised that his vision came rushing back in a great WHOOSH, and he was once again standing next to his friends, Pellonia and Arthur. He lowered the axe and the shovel. "Coffee and sweet cake? You brought coffee and sweet cake for me?"

Pellonia looked at Arthur, then back at Gurken. "Well, to tell you the truth, we started here with a sweet cake for you. But, you see, the walk back was longer than I thought it would be, and I finished mine. Since I didn't have any more sweet cake, and I was still hungry, well, I ate it." Arthur flinched and began to invoke an ancient spell of protective power, though one would be forgiven for misunderstanding his incantations and elaborate gestures as cowering and covering his face with his hands.

"Well, that's perfectly understandable," said Gurken.

"It is?" asked Pellonia and Arthur together, and at once, with a look of relief on Arthurs face and amusement on Pellonia's.

"Certainly," said Gurken, "I have often consumed more than I thought I would, but it is, as the elfs say, the thinking that is what counts."

THE BERSERKER AND THE PEDANT

Out of reflex, Arthur began "I don't think that's precisely wha... whoof." Pellonia punched him in the gut, gave a disapproving look, and grinned at Gurken.

"But then, where is this famous coffee I have been promised?" Gurken asked, smiling, an expression to which he was decidedly not accustomed, but which he found quite agreeable. "I see you have it in your hand, come pass it to me and let us be off. I brought sacks for us all to sleep in, which will protect us from the rain, too rough of terrain, and insects with a tendency to bite."

"Well then," Arthur said, "I agree, let us be off."

So it was that Gurken, Pellonia, and Arthur set off on their great adventure.

The Mines of Moog were a week's travel, when one traveled by horse. Given that it would take some time to explore the mines, recover the orb, and return from the quest, the priests of Durstin were rather surprised when Gurken returned later, if one was being generous in their description, later that evening. The priests gave the most disagreeable of looks as Gurken dumped out of the sack, and onto the temple floor, pieces and parts of Arthur and Pellonia.

"I have faith that," said Gurken to the priests, "when setting out on one's inaugural quest, one ought to be granted, as the elfs say, a mulligan."

"My Gods," the priests said, making the holy sign

of the star on their chests, "what happened?"

"Well, you see," said Gurken, " we ran into these giant ants..."

Episode Two

THE BERSERKER AND THE SLEEP SACK

"Anyone could have been killed by giant ants on the first day of their dumb quest," Pellonia remarked as she stomped through the tall, dry brush, smacking down the grass with a stick. "Stupid temple didn't have to send along babysitters."

Gimnur Hammerfist, lead babysitter, walked ahead and fell into pace next to Gurken. Gimnur was armored in elven-forged steel, though it was nicked and dinged from heavy use in battle. A thick metal shield with dents that could only have been made from something as strong as the club of a frost giant was slung from his back, and he carried a large hammer weighted for smashing. A jagged spear tip protruded from the top of his helmet, presumably used to skewer his foes when rushing into a melee, for he did not seem the type to enjoy ornamentation for ornamentations sake. Gurken had offered to share a leather sleeping sack, only to be laughed at and told that real dwarves slept on cold, bare earth.

"Gurken," Gimnur said, a friendly tone in his voice, "You're of the Stonebiter clan, eh? Tell me now, I always thought that name was a jest! A family of dwarves biting stones, the mere thought of it makes me chuckle." He chuckled, as if to accentuate his point. Gurken gritted his teeth. Now wouldn't be a good time to become wroth, having just left the city and there not being any true foes at hand. His traveling leathers had begun to chafe and Gimnur was disturbing his naturally good cheer.

"A common misconception, Hammerfist. The name was earned by my forefather for an act committed to save our king. It's a glorious name! I bade you to respect it." Gurken raised one eyebrow and his leather gloves creaked with a sound of agony as he tensed his hands. Isa, the dwarfen rune of challenge and frustration, pulsed in a low blue light on the head of his axe.

"Bade you?" Arthur whispered to Pellonia. "That's not even close! He's doing this deliberately!" Pellonia rolled her eyes. Arthur wore wizarding robes of traditional dark blue, silk, and smooth against the skin, highlighted with yellow mystical symbols embroidered along the hem. He did not wear a hat, as it was not required of his order and far too stereotypical, though out of necessity, he did wear spectacles. A sleep sack, provided by Gurken, was slung over his shoulder and stuffed with books, parchment and inks.

Throkk, assistant babysitter, shambled behind Hammerfist. Throkk was tall as a tree, if the tree

THE BERSERKER AND THE PEDANT

stood about eight feet tall. Bulky, thick black hair tufted through every opening in his clothing, and he smelled as though hygiene was not something weighing heavily upon his thoughts. He wore skins crafted from various beasts that he'd fought and slain. Whoever cleaned the skins had clearly not been overburdened with a sense of duty and took neither joy nor pride in a job well done. The juicy bits had long since dried, mind you, but they still provided a certain intimidation to those whose sensibilities included not wanting to see the insides of flesh.

"Throkk not scared of tiny Gurken dwarf and shiny axe. Throkk MASH!" Throkk glared at Gurken and mashed the ground with his club. He'd deftly crafted this club in the early hours of their long journey by uprooting a small tree and meditatively stripping the limbs and roots with his teeth as they walked. A small ant, no bigger than a breadcrumb, crawled from under his club where it had struck the ground.

Pellonia and Arthur gasped, pointing at the ant. The ant considered them, and crawled away. Gimnur and Throkk laughed at their reaction. Not a polite chuckle, no - there was a bit of pointing and clearly erroneous statements such as "I can't breathe" and impolite implications as to their valor and worthiness for the quest.

"You! You just made a BIG mistake," Pellonia

taunted. "Gurken is going to become wroth. You know he's a templerager, right? You won't like him when he's wroth! Gurken's going to tear into you with his axe and... um, apparently, savage you with the sleep sack he is taking out of his pack. Then... brutally untying. And ruth...less...ly... climbing...in?" She looked at Gurken with a mixture of anger and confusion, sprinkled with a bit of wonder and a dash of concern.

"Gurken!" she whispered, as Gimnur and Throkk thrashed on the ground in uncontrolled laughter. "What are you doing? Now isn't the time for a nap!"

Gurken, standing with an open sleep sack about his feet, dropped the sides and held out a fist towards Pellonia. He raised his thumb, "Firstly, the merchant selling these sleep sacks spoke about how they can ward off a certain degree of moisture, thus making them fit for sleeping dry even in the rain, so long as the water did not puddle underneath."

"What does that have..." Arthur began.

"Have you not learned it's unwise to interject me, wizard?"

Arthur ceased his interjection, preferring to listen to Gurken finish, rather than listen to his own voice - despite his enduring love for it - the cost would likely have been more than he wanted to pay.

Gurken raised his forefinger. "Secondly... the shopkeeper also said they would provide comfort from small rocks, a miscomfort I can attest to, having felt it often enough that small impressions are permanently etched upon my back."

Arthur gritted his teeth upon hearing the word "miscomfort"; but let no one say that wizards are unable to learn, as he said nothing.

Gurken raised a third finger. "And lastly," he smiled, "according to the good vendor, the sacks have the agreeable convenience of keeping various biting insects..."

"Such as ants?" said Pellonia.

"Such as ants, " Gurken agreed, "at bay."

"Gurken," Arthur began, having waited for a lull in the conversation so as to not inappropriately interject, "It's one tiny ant."

"As to that," Gurken said, "you are, as always, faultless in your art of perception. There is currently only one tiny ant. But, is this not the field upon which we encountered much larger ants which resulted in a certain amount of death among us? Also, wasn't the appearance of larger ants preceded by that of smaller ants?"

Throkk lifted a foot, and stomped on the little ant. It was too small to make a proper squishing sound. As if Gurken had been granted the gift of prophecy, a somewhat larger ant crawled over Throkk's foot, this one as big as a hand.

"We run!" Arthur said, staring and pointing at the ant. "We should retreat! Withdraw to fight another day, I always say."

"Run!" scoffed Gurken, "I, a templerager of the Stonebiter clan, run? I think not! You? A learned and powerful wizard run from mere ants? I think you'll not do that twice! Unless you're satisfied with how that turned out last time."

"Well, shouldn't we fight?" asked Pellonia, pulling out a blade, albeit one more appropriate to the peeling of fruit than to piercing a carapace.

"What, fight ants? Come, now what have they done to us?"

"Besides kill us?" Arthur murmured in a voice low enough to avoid interjection.

"Nope, nothing to be gained by it. There is but one thing to do. I see you are both standing there doing nothing, and it would take far too long to open your own sleep sacks and set them up. So, are you getting in here with me? I can't continue to wait for you."

Pellonia and Arthur scrambled over to Gurken, stepped in the sleep sack, and helped pull the sack up and over their heads.

Throkk and Gimnur guffawed, rolling on the ground. "Ooo, the ferocious templerager. Does he need a nap before he fights?" Gurken and his friends laced up the side of the sleep sack; Pellonia's stuck out her tongue as she threaded the tie through the holes, Arthur held the sides up high, and Gurken looked smug and smiled at Gimnur Hammerfist.

Throkk stood up and went over to look at the

THE BERSERKER AND THE PEDANT

larger ant. He raised his club, intending to strike a deadly blow and crush the beast, when it sprayed him in the face with a pulpy - and rather rank - liquid. Throkk howled in rage and crushed the ant with his club. "Tiny ant no spray Throkk! Throkk squish tiny ant like bug!" he bellowed, wiping the fluid from his eyes.

Pellonia and Gurken could no longer be seen; the sack had been bound up the side and over their heads. Arthur, having the greatest height, looked on as a pair of ants crawled out of the tall grass and into the clearing, scrambling towards poor Throkk. They sprayed foul smelling mist into the air as they came. Throkk smashed one ant with his club as Gimnur crushed the other.

"Gurken, what are you doing?" Gimnur demanded, the change in tension in his voice betraying his growing concern. "It's just a few measly ants!"

Arthur finished lacing the sack closed, and the trio, unable to coordinate their movements, promptly fell over. A dozen more ants scurried into the clearing, spraying mist in the air. The ants scrambled over the sack and charged past, towards the remaining combatants. Gimnur and Throkk made fast work of them. "Is that the best they can do? Spray us with a bit o' disgusting mist? We can kill thousands of these little buggers without breaking a sweat! Bring it on!"

As if in answer to his taunt, a sink hole opened in the ground, ten feet from Gimnur and Throkk. Dozens of small ants, and one ant of considerable size, streamed out of the hole. The ant of considerable size's head was as big as Throkk and its mandibles made loud "toch toch toch" sounds as they opened and closed.

Pellonia, peering out a tiny hole in the seam of the sack, saw Throkk and Gimnur charge the giant ant before being obscured by it. She heard the sound of a battle cry, followed by the sound of battle screaming, battle crying, and finally, battle silence.

"This is NOT our fault," Pellonia said.

"Still, we should return their remains to be mended," said Arthur.

The sack was scooped into the air, and pinchers compressed around them, trapping their arms at their sides. The giant ant brought them to the hole and dove inside.

Episode Three

THE BERSERKER AND THE ANT

Pellonia, who to all appearances was a twelve-year-old girl with chestnut pigtails, freckles, and impish little dimples woke up in the very uncomfortable and rather unfamiliar position of being pressed between Arthur and Gurken and sewn into a leather sleep sack.

"Well, THAT happened," she said in disbelief, peeping out a hole in the hem of the sack. The darkness extended beyond the confines of the sack and into the space beyond. She listened, but could not hear anything over the sound of Gurken's thundering dwarfen snores. She floundered around in the darkness of the sack until she found his beard and followed the clay-caked mat of hair up to his nose, and - the effort requiring both of her hands - pinched his nose shut. He snorted air in through his mouth and woke.

"Wha-? Where are we?" he said, smacking his parched lips. "Are there foes about?"

"We're wherever the giant ant carried us. Now shut it, you're louder than a sickly dragon. I'm trying to listen." She listened, there was nothing to be heard but the cacophony of silence. She cut the leather binding on the sack with her knife, pulled open a hole, and crawled out. She cut the rest of the leather cord, freeing Gurken and Arthur from the sack.

"What do we do now?" Pellonia asked.

Gurken stood up, stretching his legs. He was rather thrilled that the sack had worked as advertised. Though he had slept upon the earth, it had shielded him from small rocks and lumps prone to cause discomfort and disturb one's sleep, he had remained dry - though to be honest, there was little enough moisture about - and it had protected them from insects, like ants, that were prone to bite tender and exposed skin - just ask poor Throk and Gimnur.

"Seeing as we've just awoken, a coffee wouldn't be out of order," Gurken said.

"A coffee? We don't even know where we are! We can't even see!" Pellonia gestured in the dark to indicate that they could not see.

"Well, hold on, it's a tolerable temperature, we're neither too cold nor too hot. We're neither being rained on nor battered by a too hot sun. I hear no foes seeking to skewer us, and we've camped here safely through the night unmolested. Coffee necessitates fire, which will provide light, with which we can learn where we are while we brew our coffee. Shall we put this plan into action?"

Pellonia could think of no argument against, so Gurken picked up Arthur with one hand and shook him awake.

THE BERSERKER AND THE PEDANT

"What? No, please don't kill me! I didn't even say anything this time!" pleaded Arthur.

Gurken chuckled. "Wizard, we need fire. Can you magic us one?"

"Can... you... magic us one? Really, that's how you ask?" asked Arthur, plainly irritated at the rough treatment.

"Can you... magic us one... please?" Gurken said, confused.

"When one requests an invocation from a wizard, one ought deliver the request with decorum and respect. 'Esteemed wizard, we are in urgent need of a fire; perchance you might conjure one for us?'"

"Perchance you might conjure one for us?" Gurken asked, this time with irritation in his voice.

"Right, then. I'll still need some wood."

Gurken fished around in his pack and brought out some kindling which he handed to Arthur. A few moments later there was a mystical sound eerily reminiscent of flint and steel clicking together, a sorcerous crackle as dry weeds curled in the sudden heat and a warm arcane orange glow that washed over Arthur's face.

"Presto flame-o, fire! Tuh duh!"

Pellonia looked askance at Arthur, one eyebrow raised, a flat expression on her face, as if to say "No one could possibly believe that was magic."

"Well done, wizard!" Gurken declared, rummaging around for his pot and beans.

Pellonia shrugged.

Arthur looked around the chamber. It was tall and unfinished, an area of earth hollowed out by the ants for some purpose, perhaps to store food, making it a larder, to grow food, making it a sort of greenhouse, or a spot for prisoners, placing them, once more, in a dungeon. A tunnel led away from them, out of the room and into the darkness. Pellonia, facing Arthur, slowly lifted her gaze above his head, then moved her head up and up and up.

"Don't... move... an inch," Pellonia said.

Arthur looked behind him, moving rather farther than one inch, and saw a pile of eggs resembling dirty leather sleep sacks towering over him. Ah! It was a nursery then. Oh good... On the ground next to the fire, an ant the size of a kitten fell from one of the eggs in a purplish goo. It stood up, shaking itself off and scurried over to Arthur, nudging him with fierce pincers lined with razor-sharp teeth. It ticked hungrily at his flesh.

"No, no no. Shoo. Scat, go away!" Arthur brushed the ant away with the sleeve of his silken robe. It came scurrying back, its clicking sounds quickening, pincers menacing the nervous wizard.

"I said, don't move," hissed Pellonia. She pulled a salted fish out of Gurken's pack and handed it to Arthur.

"Thank you, I am rather famished, but I don't think I'll be eating just now."

"It's not for you," she snapped. "Give it to the

THE BERSERKER AND THE PEDANT

ant!" She pointed towards the insect.

Arthur handed the fish to the ant, which tore into it with the glee of a rabid creature enjoying a meal. After devouring the sardine, it scurried into Arthur's lap, curled into a little ball and fell asleep. Arthur tentatively pet the little critter; it was not all hard carapace as he had expected - there were little soft tufts of hair protruding from various places. Its pinchers flexed in pleasure and it gave out a series of soft clicks as he stroked its soft fur.

"D'awww," Pellonia purred, clasping her hands near her face and fluttering her eyelashes. "He likes you!"

A loud shriek pierced the air. Pellonia, Arthur and the ant jumped up, ready to flee should conditions require it.

"Coffee's ready!" shouted Gurken with pleasure, taking the pot off the fire and pouring out a mug's worth for each of them, hardly singeing his fingers in the process.

"Already?" Pellonia asked, "that seems pretty fast."

Gurken gave her a bemused look. "It was a magical fire, after all."

"Quite," said Arthur, smirking.

After observing their morning rituals, Gurken checked his armor and equipment to ensure everything was in its place, Arthur fed his new insectile companion and considered what to call it, and Pellonia rolled some eggs closer to the fire and tried in quite imaginative ways to get one to open for her.

"You should call it Kitty," said Pellonia, sitting on one of the eggs, "on account of its soft fur and tendency to purr."

Gurken's axe was at the ready, honed to a nearly sharp edge. He walked to the tunnel entrance and listened. Having scanned for danger with keen dwarfen senses, he gestured for them to follow.

"That doesn't quite fit him," Arthur said, walking over to Gurken "I'll have to get to know him better first."

Pellonia jumped down and walked towards them, looking mournfully back at the nest of eggs, "I'd have called mine Kitty."

They followed the corridor for some time, alert for any sign of danger, well... Gurken was alert for any sign of danger, Pellonia and Arthur were alert for any sign of a good name for the ant, which skittered about the floor, ranging ahead before getting interested in some scent on a rock and falling behind. It climbed on Arthur before settling on his shoulder and nibbling at his ear.

"Skitter!" "No." "Legs!" "No." "Anty!" "No." "Tickles!" "Hmm. No." "Pincy!" "No." "Fluffy." "I'm afraid not."

"STOP!" Gurken said.

"Sorry, Gurken," said Pellonia, "I didn't realize we were bugging you." She sniggered. Arthur chuckled.

"No, look ahead." Gurken pointed down the tunnel. At the edge of the torch light was a pair of yellow eyes on a green scaled face, forked

THE BERSERKER AND THE PEDANT

tongue flicking towards them. It slithered into the luminescence, stretching its supple shape, slipping past the soil. A snake. Easily sixty feet long, it lifted its head into the air, hissing.

"Dragon!" Arthur and Pellonia yelled, pointing up at the beast, frozen in its terrifying aura.

"Dragon!" Gurken roared with glee, raising his axe. Thurisaz, the dwarfen rune of directed destruction and masculine fervor etched upon it's head, blazed. Gurken charged, bloodlust urging him on. He swung the axe delivering a mighty blow with enough force to sever the trunk of a tolerably round tree. The snake swayed away from the blow, sparks showering the shaft. It unhinged its massive jaw, enveloping the dwarf and swallowing him whole. A dwarf sized protrusion struggled in its neck and slid deeper down its craw. It hissed in pleasure, swallowed, and turned towards Pellonia and Arthur, tongue flicking.

Pellonia and Arthur tried to move, but all of their courage could not budge them. They remained still as stone, mouths agape, pointing at the slinking serpent. It slowly slipped closer, eyes steadily staring. The snake sniffed, its tongue tasting Arthur's skin.

The ant hopped on the snake's face, landing between its eyes, spraying a sticky mist all over it. The snake shrunk aside, flinging the ant through the air, and hissed at it, muscles straining to strike. Dirt fell from the ceiling, pummeling the snake on the head, knocking it to the ground. A giant ant fell out of the hole and landed upon it with a "toch toch toch", pincers severing the snake's head from its body before the ant burrowed into the floor and out of sight. Gurken burst out of the stomach, axe glowing, eyes alight in berserk glee, shaking off stomach acid and blood. "That's disgusting!" he said, smiling. The small ant came trotting back to Arthur, who bent down to pet it.

"Antic!" Pellonia said.

"Oh, I like that one," Arthur agreed.

Episode Four

THE BERSERKER AND THE MINOTAUR

"We've been wandering for DAYS since we killed the dragon," Pellonia whined. The whine, coming as it was from a rather slight figure having the appearance of a twelve year old girl, down to the freckles, pigtails, and pouty dimples, had a rather effective pitch that carried a long distance and had the attributes of a shriek: high pitch, impossible volume, and excruciating irritation.

"Come now," said Arthur, in a annoying, upbeat manner, "what kind of attitude is that? Firstly, we've been wandering for a few hours at most, and additionally, we're, on a grand adventure! What more could one want?" Arthur stroked his charming new companion, Antic, acquired mere hours ago. Antic lay perched on Arthur's arm, warming himself in the blue silken sleeve of Arthur's wizarding robe and nibbling bits of salted cod. Pellonia glared at Antic and sighed, surrendering to Arthur's pluck and good fortune.

Arthur continued, "Gurken, we've been following you around this labyrinthine tunnel for ages. What strategy are you following to get us out of here?"

"Right."

"I do apologize, but I don't understand."

Gurken, a dwarf currently wearing the ill-fitting leather armor he favored for travel, an axe granted to him by the gods, a shovel borne for its utility, and an empty but quite versatile sleep sack, shrugged, "We're turning right."

"That doesn't exactly convey the impression of an exhaustive strategy."

"Ancient dwarfen strategy. When lost in a maze, such as this one, keep turning right until the exit presents itself."

Arthur blinked twice. "Gurken, that strategy isn't guaranteed to lead to an exit."

Gurken's bushy eyebrows furled, his mouth puckered. "Keep to your books and magicking, wizard. Dwarves know the underground and, since you're practiced in the art of perception, I believe it fair to say that you can perceive that I'm a dwarf and thus conclude that I know the underground."

"Gurken," Pellonia said, sulk giving way to mischievous grin. "Arthur's correct."

"Aha! See there!" said Arthur, pointing at Pellonia. "It's not just me; even Pellonia concurs. One cannot extricate oneself from a maze just by turning right."

"Yeah, I've heard you have to always go left." Pellonia smirked.

THE BERSERKER AND THE PEDANT

"Precisely," said Arthur, nodding, "one must always go... what? No, that is the same faulty reasoning! Logically, always turning in one direction does not work. It only makes a circle."

Gurken shook his head sadly. "Circles don't have turns."

"Fine, then! A square, it makes a square."

"Only if you always turn after an equal number of steps," countered Pellonia. "That isn't what we're proposing. It's really more of a rhombus."

"The point is..."

"No, rhombuses still have equal length sides, you're thinking of a trapezoid." Gurken interjected Arthur, quite enjoying the experience.

Arthur pinched the bridge of his nose with his fingers, closing his eyes. "The point is, there is no guarantee constantly turning in one direction will get us out of the maze; it could quite easily lead us back to where we started, which I am beginning to conclude is what has happened to us."

"What if we were to alternate?" asked Pellonia. "First left, then right?"

"No, always turn right. Ancient dwarfen saying."

"I don't mean to disparage the sayings of your ancestors, Gurken, but here, let me show you." Arthur started drawing a trapezoidish figure in the dirt while Pellonia and Gurken continued on. He was nearly finished with his proof when a stomping sound echoed down the tunnel, followed by deep angry breaths. Arthur looked, straining his eyes, and heard a sound not unlike that of an enraged bull, just before being struck in the head by two enormous horns and flung down the corridor past Pellonia and Gurken. He landed in a heap with a sickening crunch, head disjointed, and said, "They'll never find their way out in time to have me mended." Then he died.

Pellonia and Gurken had watched as Arthur sailed overhead, a resigned look on his face. They looked back down the tunnel. A beast stared back at them, a beast with the body of a man and the head of a bull. His - and it was quite distinctly a he, as the rags he wore left little to the imagination - his breath was hot and moistened the air as he breathed in and out. His eyes were narrow slits, pressed closed in fury. He held an axe with a head as big as a man's body and a shaft six feet long. He let out a long bellow of challenge and scraped a foot into the ground.

Antic, who had fallen at the beast's feet, stared down the half-man, half-bovine creature and spewed a foul smelling liquid. It struck the beast's chest, clinging to his torso and dripping to the floor. The brute retreated one step as dirt fell from the ceiling, landing where he'd stood. A giant ant as big as a horse fell to the floor, its enormous pincers closing on air. Toch toch toch. The half-man let out a low rumbling bellow, swung his axe in a mighty arc

THE BERSERKER AND THE PEDANT

and hacked the giant ant in two. Antic, obviously a creature of intelligent calculation, like his human companion, skittered away towards Arthur as the giant ant fell in half, its insides pouring outside. The half-man stepped through the middle of the corpse, feet splashing through the gore.

"I am Bratax the Wanderer - who dares enter my labyrinth?" Bratax shouted, arms raised in the air in challenge.

"Minotaur!" Pellonia shouted, pointing at Bratax. She turned left, sprinting into the maze, her feet pitter-pattering down the hall until her footsteps fell silent.

"Minotaur!" Gurken yelled, raising his axe to the heavens, or at least towards the high ceiling of the tunnel they fought within, to meet Bratax's challenge. Fehu, the Dwarfen rune of domestic cattle and hope sizzled and seared into the axe's head, branding it with power. "I dare! I, Gurken Stonebiter, templerager of the Stonebiter clan, avatar to Durstin Firebeard! I come seeking an exit, but it would give me great joy to engage you in a battle to the death! Not my death, bullish one. Yours." He pointed the head of his axe at Bratax.

Bratax lowered his enormous axe; the head was so big that this was mostly a matter of attitude while holding onto the axe, as the difference was less that an inch, but nonetheless, it was easily noticed by trained warriors. Gurken noticed it too.

"Tomaso axe?" Bratax inquired.

"Aye."

"Impressive. Why does the bearer of a Tomaso axe trespass upon my labyrinth?"

"Ants."

"Ah."

"Indeed."

"Well, then."

To continue with an exacting description of the intellectual dialogue between the two fierce warriors would tax even the most patient and studious among us. Suffice it to say that there was some grunting and gesticulating, followed by posturing, humor, and finally understanding. Rather then sit through the peace accord in its entirety, let us skip ahead.

"Why do you dwell within these tunnels?" asked Gurken.

"Some say it's because I'm thrall to a powerful wizard and guard his treasure. Some say that I protect a fair virgin in the center of the maze. Sadly, the truth is much more mundane. I'm lost."

"Lost, you say?"

"Lost. I cannot find my way out of here."

"Well, then! You are in luck, for I have some small knack for finding my way out of the underground."

"Well, then, if you do help me find the way out, I shall forever be in your debt."

"Not at all, just..."

THE BERSERKER AND THE PEDANT

"Yes?"

"Just help me carry my fine friend here, Arthur, out of the labyrinth and discover the whereabouts of Pellonia and then I would consider the debt paid."

"Pellonia? The young one that took off to the left?"

"You have it exactly."

"Ah, well, that is problematic. You see that is the way deeper into the labyrinth. She will come first to an intersection, and - why, if she goes right, then she will be lost."

"And if she goes left?"

"Well, then, if she goes left, not only will she be fine, she'll return this way in some time."

"In that case, let's sit here and enjoy the company of one another, for I have a strong suspicion that she'll come along this way. Hello, what is this?" It was at this exclamation that Gurken noticed Arthur's scrawlings on the floor and walked closer so as to better observe them. After observing they were of some import, he considered them, and upon some time spent in profound consideration, he even understood them.

"Huh. It appears one cannot just turn right."

⚔

"A centaur!?! Really? That's the best they could do?" asked Arthur, a furious scowl upon his face. He stood in the temple stable, a small building hewn from rock that had but one room. Arthur and Pellonia currently resided within, as well as some covering of hay. On the wall were some clasps, once used to secure gardening instruments, but which now held a brush with a long handle and a large file used for the shaping of hooves.

Pellonia regarded Arthur. "At least the horse half is on the bottom," she said, "and all white. Hey! You might be half-unicorn!" She squealed with delight.

"That is none too helpful."

"The priests said you've died so many times that it's getting to be a lot of work to keep mending you. They also had to mend Throkk and Gimnur and all this mending is hard on them. It was this, or nothing. Besides, it's not forever."

"What do you mean, it's not forever?" Arthur asked, his long equine tail swishing. "You mean this will wear off?" He gestured towards his white equine hindquarters.

"Well... not exactly. You see..."

"Yes?"

"Well, the next time you die, they promised to mend you up right."

"Next time? They're just assuming I'll be killed again?"

"You've died three times in the last four days. Seems a rather fair assumption."

"Hey!"

"Is for horses." Pellonia snickered. "Come now,

THE BERSERKER AND THE PEDANT

we must go to the blacksmith and get you some shoes."

Episode Five

The Berserker and the Centaur

"This is so ridiculously, contemptuously, and flabbergastingly unfair."

Arthur, in his newly mended centaur body, trotted alongside a gloriously ornamented white opaline carriage, encrusted with golden inlays, onlays, overlays, and outlays. Arthur crossed his arms in protest. Pellonia and Gurken, sitting on plush, well-cushioned velvet seats, peered out of the carriage. Pellonia stuck her arm out the window, holding a platter of sweet cakes. Antic lay upside down in the middle of the platter, covered in crumbs. A solitary treat sat unmolested where dozens had lain before.

"Duh hu wahn un?" Pellonia asked, mouth stuffed full of cake.

"Seven days! Seven days we've traveled without event! Even my hooves are sore! Who knew hooves could get sore? I didn't know, and I'm a wizard. We usually know things."

Gurken plucked the remaining treat off the tray, eating it in one gulp and swallowing with the assistance of a large stein full of mead. "You are correct, dear Pellonia, he does whine overly much." He wiped his mouth with the back of his sleeve and surrendered to a large belch.

Another face appeared from inside the carriage, the face of a nobleman. He was resplendent with gold and jewelry. "Once more, Arthur, I feel obligated to apologize. I'm very sorry, there's just not enough room in here for someone of your considerable, hmm... what's the word I'm looking for?"

"Mag-neigh-tude?" Pellonia provided.

"No, I-"

"Oat-versized? Hay-mungus? Tower-rein?"

"Enough-gh!" Arthur neighed, quickly covering his mouth with one hand. Pellonia laughed, and even Gurken smiled.

"We're here," Arthur said. "Thank the dwarfen gods, we're finally here. Observe, the entrance to the Mines of Moog."

A rusted and ruined rail track ran through a small valley between two not overly large hills, continuing into a cave dug into the side of a cliff. Weeds had grown up, over, and around the tracks, and a mining cart lay overturned, rusting in front of them. Bones of various creatures lay sorted in piles strewn about the entrance to the cave, a pile of femurs here, a pyramid of skulls there.

"Well, then," said their noble traveling

companion, "here is where we part ways, I'm afraid. Gurken, Pellonia, Arthur, you have my gratitude for allowing me to accompany you this far on your quest. I have quite the story to tell the archduchess. She will not be able to resist me after this tale of my bravery and adventure."

Our compatriots said their fare thee wells to the good nobleman, thanking him for the ride, the refreshments, and the company. They watched as he rode away in his carriage.

"I do think I'll miss his sweet cakes most of all." Pellonia sighed.

The three turned to face the mines, well aware that within they would have the chance to perform many brave deeds of daring, facing dangers unknown. Should they survive, their deeds would be immortalized in song and tales, and a powerful artifact of the temple, the Orb of Skzd, would be reclaimed. Fail, and they were far, far from any help, any aid, any succor. Die and they would remain deceased. But did they pause? Did they hesitate? Did they entertain any notion of delay on their quest?

Out of the mouth of the cave lumbered a figure so large it had to hunch over and squeeze through the opening. Small boulders were loosed from above as the cliff rumbled in complaint at the rough treatment. The rocks bounced off the creature and thudded to the ground. The hills shuddered against the creature's strength. Its flesh, swampy green and

THE BERSERKER AND THE PEDANT

moist, seeped a elven steel colored fluid out of small pustules all over its body. It's claws, as long as Gurken's legs, scraped against its fangs as it picked something out of its teeth. The creature dislodged a chunk and casually flicked it away. It landed in front of them and rolled to a stop at their feet. It was a severed hand.

"Trolls," Gurken whispered. "Arthur, perchance might you magic us a ball of flame? Or cause it to fall into a deep slumber?"

"Um, well, as to that..." Arthur stammered. "I'm afraid not."

Gurken furled his brow. "You've spent ten years in wizarding school, wizard. What did they teach you?"

"Well... mostly grammar. I'm afraid that I'm only of the tenth rank. Wizards don't get to the really good stuff for another thirty ranks or so. Besides, I don't have an orb to focus magic."

Gurken stared at the wizard, unable to comprehend what the wizard did the honor of telling him. The ground trembled as another troll pushed through the cave's opening. "Aahm ungry," it bellowed.

"Maybe," suggested Pellonia, interjecting, "we should find someplace to rest the night, and enter the mines in the morning?"

"Yup," Gurken agreed, nodding with approval a bit too quickly. "One ought not enter a dungeon without being fully rested. At the top of one's game, as the elfs say."

"Indeed," said Arthur, stamping a hoof. "Let's follow that trail up the hill and see if there is an area of sufficient comfort and discretion where we may set up camp." They scurried up the trail, taking care to remain out of sight.

After walking some distance and reaching the top of the hill, our brave adventurers came upon a tiny hovel; that is to say, a small building made of dried mud, covered with a thatch roof, and having a door constructed of twigs.

"Hullo," Arthur called. "Is anyone home?"

"Hush!" Pellonia said. "Who knows what dangers lurk within? There could be more trolls!"

"Trolls? In there?" Arthur pointed down at the hovel door. "The door can't be more than four feet tall. Don't you think a troll would build something a bit larger?"

"They could be box trolls," said Gurken.

"What's a box troll?"

"They're like trolls" - Gurken stuck one hand out flat, holding it as far above his head as he could reach - "but smaller." He moved his hand down to waist height. "They tend to live in boxes; hence, box troll."

"So, not a box troll then," Arthur said, gesturing toward the hovel.

"Oh, they could be country box trolls. It is rather

THE BERSERKER AND THE PEDANT

difficult to find a box so far out of the city."

Pellonia nodded at Gurken's wisdom.

Arthur clenched his teeth. "It's... not... a box troll," he said.

"Fine. Fine," Pellonia said. "Please, continue then, by all means."

Arthur was about to continue when a pile of twigs crested over the side of the hill. They watched the pile of twigs move toward them, its forward progression arrested by bumping into Arthur's leg. The pile grunted. A small humanoid face popped up over the bundle of twigs. Gray hair protruded from his ears and nose and surrounded his face in a peppery mane. His eyes bulged out of his head when he saw them and he gave out a yelp, throwing the twigs in the air. He was naked, though a thick tuft of hair concealed any naughty bits. And he was dirty, very, very dirty. And small, no more than two feet tall. At the most. He took off in a sprint as the twigs came raining down around them.

Before he had gotten three strides, Arthur grabbed him by the hair - on his head - and lifted him into the air.

"Box troll?" Arthur asked.

Gurken sighed. "No, this creature is remarkably more disgusting and annoying. It's a knoll dwarf."

"What's a knoll dwarf?"

Gurken frowned. "The most cultured and majestic of dwarves is the mountain dwarf, of which

I am one." Pellonia and Arthur crinkled their brows at the thought of Gurken being considered cultured or majestic. "We build our cities in mountains; hence, mountain dwarf. Hill dwarves are far rougher, uncultured creatures in comparison. They don't build cities; they build villages. Can't fit a city in one hill, you see. Knoll dwarves" - he pointed at the creature - "well, one can't fit more then a single family on a knoll. They're quite uncivilized, feral creatures. He probably has rabies."

"I don't have rabies!" said the knoll dwarf in a high-pitched squeak, swinging his fists through the air.

"He talks!" Gurken said, mouth agape.

"Of course I talk!" squeaked the knoll dwarf. "What do you think I am? A mound dwarf?"

Pellonia looked at Gurken in askance. Gurken closed his eyes and shook his head.

"Put me down!" the knoll dwarf peeped.

Arthur set him on the ground.

"What's your name?" Pellonia asked.

"Moog," he said. "I'm a mender."

"A mender?" Arthur asked. "We could use one of those." Moog grinned.

"Oh no," said Gurken, shaking his head and pointing at Moog. "I'm not traveling with that." Moog frowned, his head and shoulders drooping.

"Gurken!" said Pellonia. "Be nice!" Moog raised his head and smiled. She turned to Moog and said

THE BERSERKER AND THE PEDANT

"Moog, we're looking for an orb about yay big." She cupped her hands together. "It probably looks very valuable."

Moog just looked at her with confusion in his eyes. He scooped up a ball of mud and handed it to her, smiling.

"Ug, no. You know, an orb. A sphere? It's like... a ball. Round?"

Moog shrugged.

Gurken rolled his eyes, grabbed one of the twigs and drew a small circle in the dirt. Moog's eyes lit up.

"Yes! I know what that is!" said Moog.

"You do?" asked Pellonia.

"Yes."

"Where is it?"

"I'm not going to tell YOU."

"Why not?"

"It's mine."

Gurken, Pellonia and Arthur looked at each other. "Is it, perchance, in there?" Arthur asked, pointing at the hovel.

Moog ran to the door and hugged the hovel. "You can't go in there! It's mine!"

Arthur picked up Moog by the hair again and opened the twig door. The door broke off in his hand.

"Hey, that's mine!" shrieked Moog.

Pellonia walked inside.

"Mine, mine, mine!"

It wasn't quite dark inside, as the poorly thatched roof let in a bit of light, but one might charitably say it had a bit of dimness to it. There was nothing inside but a small pile of dirt. As Pellonia brushed it away, a bluish light peeked out of the ground, growing in strength as the orb was uncovered. Moog continued his barrage outside. "Mine! Mine! MINE!"

The orb was covered in small glowing runes. The blue light dimmed when Pellonia picked it up. It was made out of a platinum colored metal and was warm to the touch. It hummed with power and the air around it stirred. Pellonia stared at it, watching as the runes twisted, moved, and disappeared, leaving the orb a polished metal without ornamentation.

Pellonia brought the orb out with her, holding it up so everyone could see. "I think I broke it," she said.

"Mine!" yelled Moog, this time in despair. Pellonia tossed him the orb. "Here," she said.

It struck Moog in the head and dropped to the ground. He scowled while rubbing his head where it had struck.

Arthur set Moog down. Moog picked up the orb and said "Mine," grinning from ear to ear.

Gurken and Arthur looked at Pellonia. "Well, he's coming with us anyway, right? Might as well let him hold onto it if it makes him happy."

THE BERSERKER AND THE PEDANT

"Mine," agreed Moog.

"Oh no," said Arthur. He let out a loud groan. "You've got to be kidding me."

"What?" asked Pellonia.

"I've only just understood something. Gurken, what exactly did the priests say about the location of the orb?"

"Just that in order to get it, we'd have to endure the Mines of Moog. Why?"

Pellonia groaned.

"Mine," said Moog, rubbing his orb and smiling.

Episode Six

The Berserker and the Patrol

⛨

"I'm sorry," Arthur said. "But I cannot do it. It would be undignified." Arthur pranced along the path back to the village, tail swishing from side to side and occasionally lashing out to smack a fly off his ivory colored posterior. Antic slept curled up on his back, pincers vibrating in a contented purr.

"You're a centaur now! You're half-unicorn! There is nothing undignified about it!" Pellonia stomped her feet in frustration. "My feet hurt!"

"I walked seven days on they way to the mines without complaint while you luxuriated in the nobleman's carriage. You can walk," said Arthur. Gurken, walking beside his companions, raised an eyebrow at Arthur's dubious claim to have made the journey without complaint, but held his tongue.

"Arthuuuuurrrr. Carry me!" Pellonia traipsed along, dragging her feet and balancing Moog on her shoulders. Except for being two feet in height, Moog resembled a naked old man. Matted gray hair mushroomed out of the knoll dwarf's ears and nose, and he maintained a peppery mane about his head and neck. Resting his elbows on top of Pellonia's head, he grinned joyously, revealing five crooked teeth. He held the Orb of Skzd in his hands, the object of their quest.

Moog sighed, a long and happy sound. "Miiiiiiiiiiine."

"I'm sorry," Arthur said. "But as you pointed out, I'm likely half-unicorn. The first ride given by a unicorn is special - it creates a bond between the unicorn and his rider. Besides, I'm honor bound to only allow maidens upon my back."

"I AM A MAIDEN."

"Ah. Um, I see. Yes, well, that's only because you're a little girl, so that doesn't count. You must be of sufficient age that being a maiden means something. Talk to me again after you fall in love. Perhaps I'll give you a ride then."

"That's not how it works!"

"Now, now. I'm the one that's half-unicorn. What are you going to believe, some dubious tales you've heard from misinformed bourgeois, or the word of an - actual - unicorn? Nope, you're just going to have to trust me on this, that's the way it works." Arthur thrust a finger into the air, to both accentuate his point and demonstrate that it was final.

"HALT!" came a voice from in front of them.

They looked at the man who had so eloquently and concisely delivered a command that both conveyed the information he wished them to receive and had the effect he desired. Everyone halted.

The speaker was a man dressed in leather armor and a leather cloak, carrying a spear of not unimpressive length. The symbol of the village to which they were returning was painted upon his leather chest piece. Behind him were a half-dozen more people with weapons of various length.

"Who travels upon the King's Road?" he said.

Gurken took one step forward, and turned to look back at his friends. "Don't concern yourselves. I've got this."

Pellonia and Arthur hesitated, dubious of the wisdom of allowing Gurken to "get this." In the moment of their indecision, Gurken took the opportunity to proceed.

"Good sir!" said Gurken, addressing the patrolman. "It is I, Gurken Stonebiter, avatar of Durstin Firebeard, templerager of the Stonebiter clan. We've returned from our quest, in triumph, I might add in case there is any confusion on that score. We're prepared to receive all the glory and adulations that I am confident this will entail." With this, he paused, waiting for a response.

The patrolman raised an eyebrow and scratched his cheek.

"Do you have a pass?"

"I'm sorry," said Gurken. "I don't understand that which you have the honor to ask me."

"A pass. Do you have a pass to travel on the

THE BERSERKER AND THE PEDANT

King's Road?"

"Have you not heard a word I've spoken?" Gurken was becoming rather irritated. "Does one ask a hero triumphantly returning from his quest for a pass? I think not, good sir, I think not!"

"I'm afraid that I still need to see that pass."

"I see," Gurken said. He scrunched his brows in contemplation. His eyes grew wide in sudden understanding. "Yes, of course, good sir." Gurken said. "You require proof that I'm the avatar of Durstin Firebeard. Very well."

"That's not wha-" The good patrolman never got to finish his thought.

Gurken pulled out his axe and raised it above his head. Dagaz, the dwarfen rune of awareness and security, blazed upon the axe head in a fiery inferno. Flames shot into the heavens in a column of blazing glory, bathing those within its sight with a searing heat.

"Here is my pass!" Gurken said with a confident smile.

"He's got an axe!" one of the men yelled. "Get him!" yelled another.

Gurken stood there, entangled in a web of confusion. Time seemed to slow, giving Gurken the opportunity to consider.

Why are they attacking? he thought. *Perhaps they're attacking an unseen foe behind me. Well, as to that, I see no foe behind me. Furthermore, consider this arrow now impaled within my chest - either they are lousy shots or they are attacking me. Now, having presented my pass, a patrol would stand aside and allow me to pass, not attack me. Moreover, a patrol would be trained in the skill of archery and would not strike an ally unintentionally, and thus they must not be a patrol. Since they are not a patrol, then they must be brigands impersonating a patrol. Yes, that must be it. Brigands. I know well how to deal with brigands.*

Not being one to turn down a challenge or back away from a fight, or to consider such questions overly long when battle presented itself, Gurken's vision turned a glorious blood red. Time accelerated quite intensely, perhaps to make up for its previous sluggishness, but nonetheless moving ever faster with no more time for Gurken to consider.

A powerful hunger and lust for battle burned inside, and he roared in glee. Gurken raised the axe above his head and leapt towards the patrolman closest to him, flying through the air and swinging the axe in what was sure to be a mighty blow.

A fraction of a moment before the blade of the axe interspersed between the man's eyes, the patrolman was pulled backwards so that it passed harmlessly before him. The patrolman stumbled and fell to the ground, where, by all accounts, he continued to lie for the remainder of the battle.

THE BERSERKER AND THE PEDANT

Behind the patrolman stood a woman with skin of alabaster, eyes of amber, and a ponytail of jet-black hair that came down to her ankles. She wore a burgundy dress interlaced with gold ribbons. On her feet were golden sandals with cords tying them on and then wrapping up her legs. Her ears came to sharp and distinctive points. An elf.

"Little one," the elf said to Gurken. "Calm yourself, it is a simple misunderstandi-"

Gurken took a swing at the elf's neck, a strike not unlike those that had decapitated many a foe and brought many a discussion to an end. With the grace of a leaf fluttering in the breeze, the elf rolled her head to the side, her ear kissing the flat of the blade as it passed. Her arms flowed around the axe, one under and one above, and she swayed into it. The axe popped out of Gurken's hand, spun around her shoulder and came to a stop in one of her hands, pointed towards the sky.

The half-dozen patrolman turned and ran in various directions. Arthur and Moog gawked. Pellonia said, "Oh, no."

The elf smiled a crooked smile. "As I was saying, littl-"

Gurken roared and charged.

The elf, holding the battle axe with one hand on the shaft, let the head fall in an arc, using her elbow as the fulcrum. She stepped behind the axe's head just as Gurken swung at her; he connected his fist with the axe's head instead of hers.

The axe was far too heavy for the elf to use in the traditional manner of hacking and hewing, though she seemed no less effective for it. She followed the axe in smooth, supple motions. Wherever it wanted to go, she went, providing opportunities for it to turn, pivot, or swing. To those watching, it was not at all obvious which was leading and which was being led. They flowed as one.

Arthur stood, mouth agape, staring. "She's so beautiful," he said.

Moog slid off of Pellonia's shoulders and onto the ground. "So pretty," he said.

Pellonia rolled her eyes.

Gurken lunged at the elf, teeth bared and growling. The elf stepped forward into a crouch and spun to a standing position as Gurken flew by. She grabbed onto his belt with one hand, using his momentum to spin him around with her, and set him down gently on his feet facing away from her. "Show-off," Pellonia mumbled under her breath.

Incredibly confused by the sudden disappearance of his foe, Gurken whipped his head around. As he turned, the elf kept pace with his head, so that she remained out of sight.

Pellonia crossed her arms and curled one side of her lip into a look of disgust. The elf stepped back a few paces, a motion so smooth she seemed to be floating. Gurken finally spotted her and charged.

THE BERSERKER AND THE PEDANT

The elf frolicked around Gurken's exertions for several more minutes before he collapsed on the ground, panting from the exertion, his ire spent.

"Be at peace, little one," she said. "I mean you no harm." The elf knelt down beside Gurken and lay the axe on the ground. She bent over and kissed the top of his head, stood up and walked towards Pellonia.

"H-hey," said Arthur, waving.

"Moog," said Moog.

"You're such a show-off, Melody," Pellonia grumbled.

The elf smiled. "Pellonia." She breathed evenly, as if the entire affair had been a gentle evening stroll through the woods enjoying the moonlight. "Aren't you going to introduce me to your friends?"

Pellonia sighed. "This is Arthur. He's, well, he's actually a half-unicorn centaur wizard. That," she said, pointing at the panting dwarf, "is Gurken Stonebiter, dwarfen templerager. Moog is our knoll dwarf mender. We're on a quest."

"Everyone," Pellonia continued, "this... is Melody. My sister."

Gurken stopped panting, so shocked that he forgot to breathe. Arthur and Moog's mouths fell open, and the three of them spoke at once.

"You're an elf?"

Episode Seven

THE BERSERKER AND THE ELF

"Yes, fine. I'm an elf! Are you happy?" said Pellonia.

Pellonia stood in the clearing next to her big sister, the elven maid Melody. Melody was a stunning beauty; men had undoubtably fought many duels over her. Pellonia, on the other hand, looked to be a girl of twelve. She might be beautiful one day, but had not even started to come into her own. Side by side, however, Arthur could see the family resemblance, though he had yet to remark upon it.

Gurken lay on the ground, panting furiously, recovering from his... well, one could hardly call it a fight. Nor could one call it a fray, for no blows were struck. Dispute wouldn't work, either. Melody bore no disagreements with Gurken. No, Gurken lay on the ground, recovering from an "exchange" with Melody. Arthur stood beside him, hoping for an exchange of his own. With Melody, not Gurken.

"If by happy, you mean confused, then... yes," said Arthur. "How can you be an elf? Your ears aren't pointy and you don't move like... well, like that," said Arthur, delicately waving a hand in Melody's direction, as if he might displease her by acknowledging her presence. She curtsied at the compliment, winking at him.

Pellonia crossed her arms and gave Arthur a stern look. She said nothing. Arthur withered a bit under her scowl.

"Oh, she'll have pointy ears and move like me if she really wants to," Melody interjected, an interjection Arthur felt most welcome, judging by the look of relief upon his countenance. "In fact, that's why I'm here." Melody turned towards Pellonia. "It's time to come home, sis. It's time for your Awakening. The elves are leaving this world."

Pellonia's eyes grew wide. "Oh, no. No, thanks. I'm happy just the way I am. No Awakening happening here," Pellonia said, pointing at her body and forgetting all about being huffy towards Arthur. "Besides, I don't want to leave; I like it here. It's nice."

"Sorry, Pell, I don't make the rules. I'm not here to enforce them, either - just delivering a message."

"Right, then," Pellonia said. "I appreciate that. I do. I really do. But you see, I can't leave just yet. I'm in the middle of a quest."

Still lying on the ground, but having recovered a great deal of his breath and therefore able to add his two cents, Gurken began, "Middle of the quest? More like the en-" Further speech was, unfortunately, for Gurken, impeded by Pellonia's foot coming down on his face, squishing it into the mud.

"Like I was saying, I'm in the - middle - of the quest to retrieve the Orb of Skzd for the temple of Durstin Firebeard. It's quite important. Maybe, you know, after the quest is all done, I can go home for the Awakening. I'm under a geas, you know, 'mystically compelled' to recover the orb, can't leave yet. Yeah, tell Mom that after the quest, I'll be right there."

Melody laughed. "I'll tell her but I don't think she'll buy-."

Pellonia interjected, "Fine, thanks! We've got to be going now. Got to return the orb!" She lifted Moog, who was still holding tightly onto the orb, off the ground. "Can't stay, must be going! This orb won't return itself."

Pellonia put Moog under her arm and started to walk off. Arthur followed after her, waving and smiling at Melody as he went. Gurken got up off the ground, wiped the mud off his face, shrugged towards Melody, retrieved his axe and sauntered after them.

When Melody saw the orb in Moog's hand, her eyes widened. "Pell," she said, "That's not th-"

"Okay, thanks, Mel. We'll be seeing you. After the quest. After."

"But, that's not th-"

THE BERSERKER AND THE PEDANT

"Buh-bye!" Pellonia rounded the bend, still waving at Melody, and went out of sight. Gurken, Arthur, and Moog followed.

Melody smiled. "That's not the-"

"Not the Orb of Skzd!?!" Pellonia shouted. "What do you mean, it's not the Orb of Skzd? How many orbs does Moog have?"

Moog grinned. Pellonia, Arthur and Moog stood outside the Temple of Durstin back in the village. Gurken had gone inside with the orb to relay the news of the success of their quest and returned with the revelation. He handed this orb back to Moog, who kissed it and gave it a hug.

"Well, you see," said Gurken, "The priests determined, based upon their vast experience and knowledge of the subject, that this orb is lacking in several key properties the Orb of Skzd possesses."

Pellonia glared through squinting eyes. "Like what?" she said through her teeth.

Gurken held up a rolled parchment, allowing it to unfurl towards Pellonia. On the parchment was a rather handsomely drawn picture of a cube, etched with mystical symbols.

"That's a cube," Arthur noted, shaking his head. "Not an orb. Orbs are spherical." He drew a circle in the air with his finger.

"Not everyone has your knack for detail, Arthur,"

Gurken explained. "I have it on good authority that this is an accurate drawing of the Orb of Skzd. Moog, where is THIS orb?"

Moog scratched his hair-covered belly, then the top of his head. He smiled. Then frowned. Then smiled again, and finally... frowned. "Troll took it," he said, smiling again.

"Where did the troll take it?" Pellonia asked.

"Mine," said Moog, happy to have aided in the quest.

"Huh," Arthur said. "I guess 'mines' really did refer to the mines."

"Mine," Moog agreed. Pellonia glared. Gurken nodded.

"It's like I was trying to tell you, Pel." Melody came up from behind. She surprised them, not because she made a sudden appearance, but because of the way she flowed out of the environment and into their notice. It was as if she'd always been there and they were the ones intruding upon her. "That's not the Orb of Skzd, Pel. If you'd been Awakened last cycle like you were supposed to, you would've known that... I'm just saying." Pellonia glared at her.

"Then, what orb is that?" Arthur asked, pointing at the orb in Moog's hands.

"I'm not sure. Moog, dear, would you be so kind as to let me hold it for a bit?"

"Moog," Moog agreed, an enormous smile upon his face. He handed her the orb, nearly fainting as

THE BERSERKER AND THE PEDANT

his skin touched hers while handing over the orb.

Melody turned the orb over in her hands, examining it. She held it in one hand and waved her other hand over it in an intricate pattern. The orb rose from her hand, hovering in the air and glowing with a blue light.

"It's a radiant orb, an orb of light. It's nothing special, one of the five basic types." She waved her hand at it dismissively and it turned dark and fell into her other hand. "Elves learning to craft orbs practice by first building one of these. It can emit and redirect light. Sorry that it's not something more valuable. Since the priests don't seem to want it, though, its yours."

She tossed the orb towards Moog, who stepped out of the way and turned his nose up at it. The orb hit the ground and rolled to a stop just in front of Arthur.

Arthur picked it up. "Moog, if you don't mind terribly, I'd like to hold onto this orb," he said, staring at it and wiggling his fingers over it. Moog shrugged, indifferent towards his once beloved orb.

Melody smiled and removed a necklace from her neck. The necklace was a brown leather cord with a triangle pendant cut from a burgundy colored stone. "Here, Moog. I'm sorry that I took the pleasure of that treasure away from you. Let me restore that feeling with a gift." She hung the necklace around Moog's neck. He beamed with satisfaction.

"Thank you!" Moog said.

Melody nodded, turning to the rest of the group. "Well, if you don't mind too terribly, I would accompany you on the rest of your quest. If Pel does end up staying here, I may never see her again, and I'd like to spend some time with her."

"I'll give you a ride," Arthur said. "Hop on!" Pellonia looked at Arthur, mouth open wide in shock. Her face turned red and she looked positively livid.

"Pellonia," Arthur said, "can I talk to you for a minute?" He started trotted away from the group. Pellonia hurried over and caught up.

"What's wrong?" he asked.

Pellonia's scowl gave way to a frown and a tear slowly rolled down from each eye. "It's nothing," she sniffled. Arthur stopped and looked at her. "It's just... it's Melody. She's always been better at everything than I. She's prettier, she's smarter, she gets all of the attention. I mean, I love her, it's just... hard."

Arthur nodded.

"I mean, what if I go through the Awakening and I'm still not as pretty as she is, and I'm still not as smart? Look at her. How could I ever move like she does? How does she smile so much without her cheeks getting all crampy?"

"Well," Arthur said, "the ways of the elves are mysterious to me, but there is no way she is smarter or prettier than you. After the Awakening, oh boy, she'd better watch out. Her little sister might just outshine her."

"You think so?" Pellonia asked.

"I know so." Arthur nodded. "You'll just have to trust me on this; I'm half-unicorn. We know such things."

"Oh, very well." Pellonia smiled weakly.

"Also, you may want to consider being nicer to Melody. She's leaving this world, possibly forever. You won't know what you're missing out on until you've lost her, and if you don't go with her, it will be too late."

"Yeah, you're probably right," Pellonia said begrudgingly.

"Tell you what... hop on." He gestured with a thumb towards his back.

Pellonia's eyes grew wide in excitement. A big smile grew on her face.

"Really?"

"Really."

"Really, really?"

"Really, really."

"Really, really, rea-"

"Stop talking and get on before I change my mind."

Pellonia clapped her hands, then reached up. Arthur hoisted her up by her waist and set her on his back. Arthur, the half-unicorn centaur wizard, gave his first ride to Pellonia, the innocent elven child. She was positively glowing as they returned to the group, sitting astride Arthur, no radiant orb required.

"Hey, you offered me the ride," Melody said, smiling.

"Sorry, Melody," said Arthur. "This seat's taken." Pellonia wrapped her arms around his neck and gave him a squeeze.

Episode Eight

THE BERSERKER AND THE TROLLS

"Gurken," said Arthur. "It really would assist the quest if you would deign to mount the horse." Arthur stomped a hoof in frustration, his long white tail swishing from side to side. He stood just outside the corral of a horse trader, holding onto the reins of a horse. The horse looked bored.

Gurken shook his head.

"Come on, Gurken, it'll get us back to the mines faster," said Pellonia, sitting on Arthur's back, grinning stupidly and petting Antic. Soft clicking sounds came from the ant as it purred appreciatively.

Gurken continued shaking his head, lips pursed.

Melody sat on another horse, a chestnut brown mare with white socks. "It will only be for a short time," Melody said. She smiled.

"I'm afraid not," Gurken replied. "Dwarfs and horses don't get along. I'd sooner eat one." Moog, the knoll dwarf mender, peeked out from behind Gurken, eyes wide with fear. "Don't worry, Moog," Gurken said, patting him on the head. "We're not riding one of those beasts. We'll have to get a carriage."

"There are no carriages in the entire village," Melody said. "It's not like we're in a large city. If we had the Orb of Skzd, I could open a portal and we'd be there."

"If we had the Orb of Skzd," Gurken replied, crossing his arms, "we wouldn't need to go there to get it."

Melody smiled. "If you won't get on a horse, I'm afraid you'll have to walk. It's only a seven day ride."

"Walking suits me fine. If Arthur's walking, so can I." Gurken shouldered his pack and started walking.

-- Fourteen days later --

"There. That's the cave where the trolls came out," Pellonia said. They peeked through the bushes down the narrow canyon, looking past an overturned mining cart. Rusting tracks ran into the tunnel. The sun was overhead, beating down on them. There was no sign of the trolls.

"Now," said Gurken. "Here's the plan..."

"Gurken," Melody interjected, smiling and speaking gently. "I've been around for over a hundred years - you've been alive for, what? A few dozen at most? I'll come up with the plan."

"But..."

"If I might interject," Arthur said. "I do believe

THE BERSERKER AND THE PEDANT

Melody has a point, my dear fellow. Perhaps we should take advantage of her experience while she is with us."

"But..."

Moog ran over and wrapped his arms around Melody's leg. "Moog," he purred, rubbing against her.

"Fine," Gurken said, "let's hear this famous plan of yours. Then we shall see."

"Thank you," Melody said. "Since we are facing a small number of large foes, we should prevent them from fully exiting the cave, and strike them from a distance. Gurken, you and I shall take point, endeavoring to prevent them from exiting. Moog, stay behind us, ready to mend. Arthur, Pellonia, climb up to the top of the cliffs and find some large rocks to push over on the trolls."

"Ridiculous!" shouted Gurken.

"Sounds great," said Pellonia.

"Yup, it's good to have an actual plan for once. I'm in," Arthur agreed.

"Moog," said Moog, nodding.

"What?" Gurken asked, incredulous. "Fine, but it's a terrible plan."

"Gurken," Melody said. "Why, I'm surprised at you. Are you pouting?"

"I'm not pouting."

"I know pouting; I've got a little sister."

"Hey!" Pellonia said.

"See... pouting."

"Let's do this," Gurken said. Arthur, with Pellonia riding on his back, trotted up the path to the top of the cliffs. Gurken and Melody waited a time, then walked to the cave opening.

"Oh, my!" Melody said, in a melodramatic tone. "Whatever shall I do? I'm lost and alone!" Gurken curled his mouth in disgust at such a ridiculous tactic. He took the axe off his back and stood at the ready.

They heard movement from within the cave. A large humanoid shadow flickered across the canyon wall. Gurken gritted his teeth and smiled. Melody swung her arms in a wide circle and crouched into a low fighting stance, her hands balled in to fists with two fingers on each pointing out.

"HAAARR!" Gurken growled in a deep baritone.

"YAH!" Melody gave a sharp bark.

A small reddish figure emerged from the cave opening. He was dressed in brown leather rags and had a long pointed nose, too large for human proportions. His ears were large and pointed on the top and bottom. He had two rows of sharp teeth in a mouth turned up in a large grin. He raised a wooden staff with two large feathers on the end and yelled in a high-pitched scream, "Now!"

"Goblins!" Moog said, his eyes growing large as dozens of goblins poured out of the cave opening. He gave a yelp and dove into the bushes.

THE BERSERKER AND THE PEDANT

Nauthiz, the dwarfen rune of self-reliance and recognition of one's fate, glowed, a bright yellow halo around the head of Gurken's axe. Gurken charged the goblins, hacking off limbs and hewing heads from shoulders, cutting a bloody swath through the oncoming horde.

Melody side-stepped the lead goblin, catching his arm as he stumbled by and swinging him around into the next, sending them tumbling into a third. She dove over another pair, pulling knives out of the goblins' belts as she passed and throwing them into the guts of two more.

Rocks rained down from above, striking several more goblins in the head, knocking them to the ground. The goblin with the staff stood at the mouth of the cave, waving the goblins on. Dozens more streamed out of the cave. One struck Melody in the leg with a club in an incredibly lucky blow, spinning her off-balance. Another clubbed her in the face as she fell, but she spun with the blow, matching its momentum and avoiding most of the damage.

She rolled back out of reach. "Too many of them!" she shouted. "Gurken, pull back!" Gurken cut down another half-dozen goblins, not hearing Melody over the thundering of his rage. Another dozen goblins came, overwhelming Gurken and piling on top of him. Before Melody could react, Pellonia screamed from above on the cliff. Melody jerked her head up, but couldn't see anything. She ran toward the cliff face, stepped on a goblin's head and jumped ten feet up.

She caught a small outcropping with one hand, and in a motion reminiscent of water flowing down a river, she climbed. With one final effort, she leapt from the cliff, flipped in the air and landed with a tuck and a roll up on her feet, ready to do battle.

Melody paused as she saw Arthur, tiny spears protruding from his flanks, lying on the ground, a front leg broken. He held up the orb, projecting brief but intense flashes of light at dozens of small goblins, blinding and startling them.

Antic balanced on top of his back, spraying goblins that made the ill-considered decision to approach. On the ground between Arthur and the cliff was Pellonia, unconscious and trapped in a net. Melody cocked her head to one side and sighed. She sprinted over to Pellonia.

"Thank the gods you're here, I can't hold them off much longer. There ar-" Arthur began.

"I'm sorry, Arthur." Melody said, frowning. She picked up Pellonia, net and all, and slung her over her back. She ran off.

Arthur was stunned.

Come now, thought Arthur. *It's probably for the best. At least this way Pellonia will live, and with a spot of luck once the goblins overrun me, why, I shall waken once more in my own body. However, let us not go fondly into the cold night, but fight on.*

THE BERSERKER AND THE PEDANT

If these goblins want my hide, come now, I shall make them a time of it.

A goblin broke off from the pack and charged Arthur. He was about to lunge into a devastating thrust, when Arthur sent sharp flashes of light towards the goblin's eyes with the orb. The goblin came to an abrupt halt and fell to his knees, rubbing his eyes.

This just will not do, Arthur thought. *Blinding and dazing the goblins does have some effect, but that effect wears off in too little time and they once more come at me. If they decide to all come at once, why, I don't think I shall survive. I must figure out how to do more with this orb of light besides flicker a few sparks in their eyes. Come now, what else can one do with mere light?*

Antic sprayed another two goblins that started for them, and tried spraying a third, but the juice came out in a small spurt. No giant ants came to the rescue, no doubt since they were so far from the ant nest. Antic retreated and hid behind Arthur, quivering.

What types of light are there? Well now, there is light coming off a torch, lighting a room and providing some heat. There is light of the iridescent blowfish, a soft luminescence that, while pleasant on the eyes, does not seem to be of much use under this circumstance. There is also the light of the sun, a light which given enough time can cause a surface to heat up to a considerable level of discomfort.

A somewhat larger goblin, perhaps as tall as a dwarf, came out of the pack and roared at Arthur. The goblin swung an enormous mallet over its head and sent it crashing into the ground in challenge.

Arthur raised up the orb, pressed his finger to it and spoke an incantation to adjust the way the orb absorbed and discharged light. He pointed at the face of the large goblin and said "Lux trabem!" A solid beam of light, as concentrated and small as a fist, burst from the face of the orb, searing into the goblin's face. The goblin's face sizzled and burned, wisps of smoke rising as the goblin screamed in pain.

"Nice!" Arthur exclaimed. "Take that, goblin. The next one coming will really get it!" Arthur turned a section of the orb, which made clicking sounds as it turned.

click... clicK... cLicK... CLicK... CLiCK... CLICK...

The goblins stood back, looking unsure of what to do. So Arthur, gentleman that he is, decided to help them decide by providing them with a better argument.

"Intentoque lux trabem!"

The area around Arthur dimmed as streams of light poured into the orb. A single narrow point of light no bigger than a finger shone out of the orb and through one of the goblins. The goblin looked down

THE BERSERKER AND THE PEDANT

at the beam with a curious expression until Arthur moved the beam, jerking it through the rest of the goblin horde. The top half of the goblins in the front row slid off the bottom halves and landed on the ground with a sickening splut. The goblins immediately behind them fell over, groaning in pain or dead.

The goblins behind them concluded their contemplations, remembering they had plans elsewhere and were unable to continue to entertain Arthur, no matter how rude it was to abandon their guest. In short, they ran.

"Well, now," said Arthur, out of breath and still bleeding profusely. "This orb is a wondrous thing, indeed. Melody was, I think, mistaken. At least now, should my compatriots find me, I'll become a whole man again. It's almost a pity. I was becoming rather used to being a half-unicorn centaur wizard."

He slumped to the ground, the orb too heavy for his weakening arms to continue holding. The orb dropped out of his hand and rolled towards the goblins. A goblin stepped forward and said, "Well, now, who do we have here?" and smiled an evil grin.

"Whom," Arthur said. "Whom do we have here." Then he died.

Episode Nine

The Berserker and the Goblins

As the morning sun crested the horizon, shining bright light into the canyon, Moog the Mender peeked out of the bushes, wary for any signs of impending death. Goblin corpses littered the landscape. Nothing moved. He poked one foot out, nearly touching the ground with it, and jerked it back. Moog peeked out of the bushes again, still wary for any signs of impending death. Goblin corpses still littered the landscape. Nothing moved.

Moog strode confidently out of the bushes and walked among the corpses, searching quite diligently. Near the entrance to the mines, Moog found a particularly large trail of goblin corpses. On the ground, he found Gurken's sleep sack, covered in blood. There was no other sign of the dwarf.

Moog shouldered the sleep sack and made his way up the trail to the top of the cliff. He saw Arthur's corpse, unmoving on the ground, Antic nudging gently at his hand. Moog's eyes grew wide, and he ran over to him, pressing an ear against Arthur's chest. After a moment, Moog threw his arms around him, crying. Moog stayed like that for some time before sniffling and raising his head. He spotted the orb, lying a few feet away.

"Orb!" Moog shouted, smiling.

He walked to the orb and picked it up, cradling it and giving it kisses. He walked back to Arthur and fiddled with the orb. Sections of the orb twisted and turned in Moog's hands. A bluish beam streamed out of the orb in a horizontal line. Moog ran the line back and forth across Arthur's corpse a few times. As the beam passed over his body, the area around the line became momentarily transparent down to his bones.

Moog rubbed the orb and poked at it and said, "Herleven."

A pillar of light descended from the heavens, striking the ground next to Moog and Arthur's corpse. At first, nothing happened, then a speck in the center of the light appeared and grew. It grew to the size of a pea, then a pebble, then a small ball. It looked like a tiny fetus, half-human, half-horse. It quickly grew and aged through infancy, toddlerhood, childhood, and young adulthood and finally, stopped at adulthood. It was a perfect replica of Arthur.

"Moog, dear lad," Arthur said, his voice soft and weak. "You saved me. You have my gratitude." Arthur tried to stand, noticed he was still a centaur, and fell back to the ground.

"Well, if that doesn't just beat all," he said.

Gurken woke up in a dimly lit cavern. He opened his eyes and saw ropes hanging from the ceiling, hundreds of them. Some hung down a few feet; others reached the floor. Each rope was thin and fraying, and had knots tied in them every few inches. Some ended in a large knot, others without them. The ropes swayed in a gentle, mesmerizing pattern.

Gurken sat up; he was fully armored, and his axe lay next to him. The room had roughly hewn rock walls, and the floor was a natural cave floor. Stalagmites rose from the floor towards the ceiling. A small pool of water puddled in a bowl-shaped indentation next to him.

Gurken smelled the water and took a small sip. It seemed fresh, so he availed himself of it, drinking deeply. When he finished, he saw in his reflection a small cord tied into his beard. The rope had a succession of knots tied so close together that it made the rope appear to be thicker than it was. His hair intertwined with the cord, so he left it to remove later.

Gurken stood up and picked up his axe. There seemed to be only one way out of the room. He brushed many ropes aside as he walked towards the doorway. Through the doorway, he saw another room, with someone in a wooden rocking chair

THE BERSERKER AND THE PEDANT

facing away from him and towards a fire pit. There was a goblin on each side of the doorway, guarding it.

Gurken took his axe and made short work of the two goblins, cleaving their heads from their bodies almost before they could react. The chair in front of the fire pit started rocking, and the person in it hummed an unfamiliar tune. Unfamiliar, but unmistakably a gentle bedtime melody. Gurken crept around the side of the room to get a better look at whoever was sitting in the chair.

It was an older female goblin, gray scraggly hair combed neatly on her head. She wore a shawl and a dress with a print of flowers. In her hand was a length of cord. She hummed a tune as she spun it together by hand. Gurken watched her, waiting.

"Well. Hello there," she said. Her voice had the familiar cadence of a grandmother greeting her grandchildren. "Aren't you just the fiercest dwarven warrior?" The chair creaked as she gently rocked in it. "Finally woken up from your slumber, I see. Fine way to greet Gr-ma, killing her nurses. Where are your manners? Oh, but where are mine? Would you like some tea?"

Gurken lowered his axe, unsure of what to do.

The kindly old goblin took a kettle off the fire and poured tea into two small cups. "It's herbal, I'm afraid. Not much real tea around these parts." She handed Gurken a cup, and smelled her own and took a sip. She sighed contentedly.

"That's a good cup of tea, nonetheless. Do you know the secret to a good cup of tea? Let it sit for six minutes. Take the tea too soon, and it's weak. Not enough oomph to it. Not enough kick! Take the tea too late, and it's too bitter. It's overwhelming. Let it sit just right, and there is nothing more pleasing."

She hummed the gentle melody and sipped her tea for a time. Gurken stood there, holding the mug in one hand and axe in the other. Finally, she set the tea down. "Come over here so I can see you better. These old eyes aren't as good as they used to be."

Gurken walked in front of the goblin and let her have a look at him.

"Well, now, you look sharp young fellow." She gave the cord intertwined with his beard a short, sharp tug. It stung. "Stop complaining, that didn't hurt much. Nice and tight. Good, maybe you'll remember next time you start killing things." Gurken was confused.

She took the cord that she had been working on and started tying it into Gurken's beard. As she tied the first knot, she said, "This is Na. He was two years old. He has thirteen children. Na is lying over there by the room you came from, the tombs. He's dead. Who will teach his children how to act now? Who will teach them to behave? No one, that's who. If they survive the trolls, they'll be young hoodlums for sure."

THE BERSERKER AND THE PEDANT

Gurken felt a stab of pain as his beard interweaved with the knot. "There," she said and began a second knot. "This is Gra," she said as she tied the knot. "He was three years old. He has twenty-three children. Most of his are old enough now to be on their own and grew up with a father, a rarity among goblins. Sadly, they were all killed yesterday." She stared at Gurken and tugged the other knot in his beard, sending a fresh stab of pain through his face.

Finished with the knot, she stood up. "Come here now, help an old lady out." Gurken came over to the old goblin and set down his axe. She grabbed his arm and held onto it for support as she walked towards the tombs. She was arthritic, and pain clearly stabbed at her with every step, so progress was slow, giving Gurken time to consider.

He thought about Na and Gra, and about their many children. "They attacked us," Gurken said, unsure about why he should feel the need to justify his actions to her.

"Hush, child. I don't show you this to chastise you. I want you to understand the results of your actions. Everything you do has consequences. For Na and Gra, their actions have resulted in two knots. You did help out a bit with that, but it doesn't mean it's entirely your fault."

She continued to shuffle over to the tombs. Gurken looked again at the room. The ropes swayed from the ceiling. Hundreds upon hundreds of them, with thousands upon thousands of knots. "Why do some of the ropes have a knot at the end?" he asked.

"Each rope represents a family line. Each knot a death. The knot at the end of the rope represents the death of the last member of a family. No need to add more rope, so I tie it off with the last knot. Don't worry, young one, your assault upon our home represents only the smallest of contribution to the knots."

"How long have you been keeping track?" Gurken asked.

"How long? Let's see now. About nine years. Three generations. We split off from another family then. Our family had grown quite large. Those were good times. In the last few years, we've been plagued by Maro, Blod, and Boan, three great trolls."

"I've seen them. They look quite formidable."

"Aye, they are. They healed from any injury we could cause them. They wade into the goblin horde, swinging their claws and biting off our heads. We're no match for them. They don't just hunt us for food, or for sport. They have some other plan in mind for us. After killing their fill of us, they scoop up as many goblins as they can fit in enormous bags and wander off. We never tied knots for them, hoping they would return. We haven't been able to discover why the trolls took them, and I'm afraid that we never will."

THE BERSERKER AND THE PEDANT

"Why is that?" Gurken asked.

"They came last night after you killed so many of our remaining warriors and made quick work of the rest of us. We're no more. I'm the last goblin of this family now. When I die, we die. The tombs will be all that remain of us, swinging knots in a cave."

She fell silent. There was no sound save for the creaking of ropes.

Gurken said, "For my part, I'm sorry. I didn't know."

"Those that kill rarely give much time to consider consequences," she said. "Help me back to my chair, I am seven years old, and I have little time left. I would die next to my fire in my home, singing the songs of my family. Songs that will never be sung again. Come, sit with me."

Gurken helped the kindly old goblin back to the fire, and poured her some more tea. He sat with her while she sang the songs of her people. She sang through the day, stopping at sundown. She lay in the chair, breathing shallow breaths as the last of her strength ebbed away. Finally, she stopped. Gurken tied a knot at the end of the cord in his beard and wept.

Episode Ten

The Berserker and the Pedants

"Nooooooooooooooooooooo," Arthur said, pausing to take a breath, "ooooooooooooooooooooooooooooooooo."

Arthur waved his hands towards his posterior. "Why, pray tell, if I'm resurrected, do I still have the lower half of a horse? The priests promised I would be human when I next came back from the dead!"

"Oh," said Moog. "Not 'resurrect,' you want 'reincarnate.' That easy!"

Arthur slapped his forehead with his palm and sighed. "I don't suppose you know how to mend me back into a human?"

Moog scratched the top of his head and stuck out his upper lip. He closed his eyes in concentration. His eyes flew back open, and he pointed a finger in the air. "Ah! Moog know!"

"And you didn't mention this before now?" Arthur asked.

"You not ask. I do now. Arthur feel nothing," Moog assured him.

Arthur grimaced at the linguistic butchery. "'You

won't feel a thing,' Moog."

Moog looked confused. "No, Moog won't feel a thing. Arthur feel nothing, too."

Arthur sighed. "Well, let's get on with it."

Moog picked up a goblin spear from the ground and walked towards Arthur. Arthur scrunched up his eyebrows and looked at Moog.

"Whatever are you doing with that spear?" Arthur asked.

"Hold still, I kill you again. Reincarnate easy!"

Arthur's eyes grew wide, and he backed away, holding out his hands. "Moog, that's not what I thought you meant! I thought you sai-" and his rear hooves came down on open air. His eyes grew even wider as he slipped off the cliff, falling.

Moog and Antic looked over the edge of the cliff, straining their necks out, looking down. Then they looked at each other. While it was not easy to see the ant's mood from an expression on its chitinous face, its pincers quivered, which Moog took as a sign of growing irritation. Moog smiled and held up a finger, in order to ask the ant to bide some time. Moog walked back to Arthur's first corpse, slid a few sections of the orb around and said "Herelvern!"

A pillar of light descended from the heavens, striking the ground next to Moog and Arthur's corpse. At first, nothing happened, then a speck in the center of the light appeared and grew. It grew to the size of a pea, then a pebble, then a small ball. It looked like a tiny fetus. It quickly grew and aged through foal, weanling, yearling, and colt and finally, stopped at adulthood. It was a unicorn.

The unicorn's eyes grew wide, and it shook its head from side to side. It sat down on its haunches and raised its two front hooves, staring at them. The unicorn's eyes grew wide, and it whinnied in shock. Moog's eyes grew wide, and Antic cocked its head to one side.

"Oops," Moog said.

The unicorn whinnied, and its tail swished from side to side. Those well trained in the equine arts would have seen a depth of agitation and annoyance in its face.

Moog pushed at the orb a bit and said, "Herleven."

Another pillar of light formed over the seated unicorn and raised it off the ground. It tried tried to run, hooves flailing about, unable to find purchase. It continued to lift in the air, hooves swimming. The unicorn picked up velocity as it rose into the heavens. Another fetus appeared in the middle of the light and quickly grew from infancy to adulthood. Arthur sat there, naked as Moog but fully human.

"Moog, dear lad," Arthur said, his voice soft and weak. "You saved me. You have my gratitude." Arthur stood up and looked down, observing that he lacked the number of legs to which he'd become acquainted. He smiled an enormous smile, then covered himself with his hands, acutely aware of his lack of clothing. He stood up and walked over to his corpse, rifling through his pack. "I've kept a spare set of clothing with me, anticipating this very occasion!" He took out a set of wizarding robes and put them on.

"Did it hurt?" Moog asked.

Arthur considered. "If you mean did the goblins stabbing me with their spears hurt, then yes. If you mean did the resurrection hurt, then no. I remember the goblins stabbing me, dying, and the next thing I remember is waking up here."

"See," Moog said smugly, "Arthur feel nothing."

Arthur sighed. "It's 'You felt nothing,' Moog," Arthur corrected. "You shouldn't speak to someone in the third person, it's awkward. We'll make a grammarian out of you yet." Moog looked confused.

"In any event, thank you, Moog. You're an excellent mender. You even remembered to turn me back into a human." Moog smiled.

"Let's go see about our good friend Gurken, and then having found him, we shall come up with a plan to find our dear Pellonia. She can't have been taken far."

It was night when Pellonia awoke. She was lying next to the fire, extracted from the confines of the net. She heard voices, so she lay still, pretending to be unconscious.

"These 'goblins' make for exceedingly poor fighters. We need hardier stock," said a male voice.

"It seems cruel," Melody said.

"There are too few of us; we'd die off rather quickly if we fought ourselves."

"But sending others to do ou-"

"That's why we made them, Melody."

"That's not relevant, Leon. They're alive; what right do we have to conscript them?"

"Perhaps none. Perhaps this is immoral, but I won't have us die off. Neither would the All-Mother. You'll feel the same after the third Awakening."

Melody sighed.

Pellonia heard a sound of something hard cracking, followed by a tearing sound. It couldn't have come from more than twenty feet away. She risked peeking open one eye and saw Melody sitting on a log on the other side of the fire talking to a man. He was tall and lanky, and had pointed ears. Another elf. He was tinted orange, and dark shadows danced around him from the flickering firelight. If they took any notice of the sounds, they didn't react.

"We should at least prepare people for the arrival of the Phage before we go," Melody said.

"We've done all we can," said Leon, shaking his head. He looked sad. "Their fate is their own."

THE BERSERKER AND THE PEDANT

Pellonia slid silently away from the firelight. Moving deliberately, first she moved one hand, then she slid her body, then the other hand and her legs. She made her way out of the firelight and into the bushes unnoticed. Peeking through to the other side of the bushes, she saw three enormous dark figures.

They were sitting in the moonlight, back-to-back-to-back in a small clearing. Sitting down, they were still taller then Pellonia. It was the trolls.

"Maro, give us anotha," said one.

"Anotha, comin' up." Maro reached a clawed green hand into an enormous writhing bag and pulled out a small humanoid creature.

"A goblin," Pellonia whispered.

It wriggled and squirmed as Maro stretched the arm holding the goblin behind him and handed the goblin to the other troll. The other troll lifted the goblin into the air and dipped its head into its mouth as the goblin screamed and struggled, followed by a sickening crunch, followed by silence, then chewing.

Pellonia gagged at the gruesome sight as blood leaked out of the troll's mouth. The troll let out a groan of satisfaction. Pellonia took out her knife and started to crawl into the clearing when Leon burst in a few feet away.

"Blod! Put down the goblin!" he said in an authoritative voice. "They're not snacks. We need as many of them as we can get. We can't spare a single one. Maro, put the sack down, and the three of you come with us. Pellonia's disappeared, and we've got to find her."

"D'oah," Blod said, sounding rather disappointed. "Can't I 'ave one more?"

"No."

Blod threw the goblin's body over into a small pile of headless goblins and reached into the bag, pulling out another squirming goblin and biting its head off.

"Now you've done it, Blod," said Leon. He unsheathed a sword, and three orbs flew off his back and shoulders, hovering a foot above his head. One burned, flames licking at the sides of the orb. One shimmered, a coat of ice solidifying around the orb. One crackled, lightning coursing through the orb.

The other two trolls backed away from Leon. Blod roared, his mouth a gaping maw. Small pieces of flesh and flecks of blood flew towards Leon, but he stepped to the side quicker than Pellonia could see, and the bits passed by without striking him. The orbs kept pace with Leon, hovering just overhead.

The clearing flashed as lightning arced out of one orb and seared into the troll. The smell of burned flesh filled Pellonia's nose as Leon's sword bit into the troll's arm. He was only a step behind the lightning strike. The troll's arm fell from its body. Then its other arm fell away, followed by its legs and head as Leon moved in a blur. The troll's body fell to

THE BERSERKER AND THE PEDANT

the ground, revealing Leon, facing away from Pellonia, crouching with the sword facing out at the end of a swipe. Blood dripped from it.

Leon stood and wiped his blade clean with a cloth. He sheathed the sword as the orbs descended and landed on his shoulders and the back of his neck.

"Maro, Boan, let's go find Pellonia while Blod heals. And no more goblin snacks."

"Yes, masta. Of course, masta," the trolls stammered, lumbering out into the forest. Leon waited for Melody to walk up to him and offered her his arm. She took it, and they walked away.

Pellonia waited, hidden.

After some time, she heard a voice.

"There is no way that little ant is going to find her. He's just going back to his nest; we've got to come up with some other way to find her."

Pellonia heard a soft clicking sound at her feet. She looked down and saw Antic, rubbing its head against her boot. She reached down and picked up the ant, petting its head.

"It's good to see you too, Antic," she said. "I was getting quite worried."

Gurken walked into the clearing, Arthur and Moog at his side. Pellonia stepped out and ran over to Arthur. She threw her arms around him.

"There you are. We've been worried sick about you," Arthur said.

"We've got to help them," Pellonia answered, arms still wrapped around Arthur. "I don't care if they're goblins, we can't let the trolls bite their heads off and we can't let Leon take them away and make them fight when they don't want to. It's not all right."

"Just a moment, slow down," Arthur said.

"What did you say about goblins?" Gurken asked, an angry expression on his face. Algiz, the dwarfen rune of the protective urge to shelter others, burned into his axe's head.

Episode Eleven

The Berserker and the Rescue

Arthur turned the sack of goblins upside down; nine little goblins came tumbling out, falling over each other and tumbling to the ground. There was a sharp snap as they scrambled to get up. One of the goblins accidentally stepped on another's neck. Eight little goblins stood in a circle, staring at their now dead comrade.

"Oh, no!" said Pellonia.

"What've you done?" asked Gurken, furrowing his brow.

Arthur looked confused and waved a hand towards the creatures. "They're just goblins. As I recall, we killed quite a few of them yesterday. Also, I beg of you to remember, they did - actually - kill me."

"Arthur, you do need to learn to let go. Do all wizards hold a grudge like this or is it just you?" said Pellonia. Arthur scrunched his face in consternation.

"That was yesterday," Gurken chastised. "Today we know better. Goblins are people too. We're going to rescue them."

One goblin, having evidently come to the end of his string of courage, took off at a run. Not possessing the wherewithal to determine an appropriate direction for flight, he ran directly into Gurken's axe, impaling it into his head. Gurken's eyes grew wide, and his mouth fell open.

"Not the hardiest of creatures," Arthur remarked. Gurken and Pellonia glared at him.

Seven little goblins took off running in all directions. One tripped over a branch, striking his head upon a large rock. Six little goblins disappeared into the forest.

"The little buggers are rather difficult to keep alive, aren't they?" Arthur observed. "Shall we give chase?"

There was a single thumping sound in the direction one of the goblins fled. They ran over and saw that the poor goblin had run directly into a tree and lay slumped on the ground with his face squished against the tree. Five little goblins ran through the forest.

"Every life is precious," Arthur mocked, pointing a finger in the air.

"Split up and go catch one," Gurken said. Arthur, Pellonia, Gurken and Moog split up and pursued the survivors.

Gurken found one first. He carefully held his axe away from the goblin, but this caused no little bit of fright to the poor creature, who assumed Gurken

THE BERSERKER AND THE PEDANT

was preparing to swing the axe. The goblin keeled over in shock, falling backwards to the ground. Four little goblins remained. Another goblin smacked into the axe, decapitating himself, as Gurken held the axe out behind him. Three little goblins.

Pellonia chased a goblin through the forest, but the goblin was overcome by exhaustion and died. Two little goblins. Moog found one crouched behind a fallen tree, but it died of fright at the sight of Moog's furry mane lurking over him. One little goblin.

Arthur found the last little goblin. It was crouching on the ground, holding a stick and hiding behind it. Arthur reached down and picked the goblin up by its ankle. It squirmed and struggled upside down before evidently deciding to play dead, as it hung limp with its tongue sticking out, making dying sounds. Arthur returned to the clearing.

A short time later, they stood around the clearing in a circle, looking at the lone goblin survivor. The goblin was now wearing Gurken's helmet, with straw stuffed into it in order to both add cushioning and provide for the goblin's smaller head.

Pellonia donated a shirt to the "keep the goblin alive" cause, which the goblin was now wearing. The shirt was stuffed so full of dried grass that tufts of straw stuck out of the neck and sleeves. The shirt was tucked into an undergarment provided by Arthur, which was secured at the top with a bit of rope and tied around its ankles at the bottom. The undergarment was stuffed full of leaves.

Pellonia handed Gurken's shield to the goblin - well, she propped it up against the goblin anyway. "There," she said. "That ought to keep you safe." She patted the goblin gingerly on the helmet, which slid to one side. Pellonia straightened it.

"Well," said Arthur. "Now that we've rescued - this - goblin, what should we do next?"

"We still haven't found the orb," Pellonia said. "Has anyone seen it?"

Gurken shook his head. "I searched the mines and it wasn't there."

"It wasn't up on the cliff," Arthur said.

"Moog," said Moog while scratching at his beard.

There was a quiet rustling, though no one seemed to notice but the goblin. The goblin turned - well, more like pivoted on one foot, and saw the arm of the troll that Leon had hacked apart pulling itself along with its fingers. The goblin's eyes grew wide, and it pivoted back towards the group, wildly vibrating its arms trying to get their attention. He couldn't move very well, constrained as he was by all the straw stuffing, baggy clothes, and oversized helmet.

"Perhaps the trolls took the orb," Arthur said. "We'll have to track one down and ask."

THE BERSERKER AND THE PEDANT

The troll's arm succeeded in pulling itself over to the troll's torso. It set itself back in place, and the flesh between the two grew and stitched together.

"Ask a troll?" Gurken said. "I hardly think they are the most talkative of creatures."

Another arm connected on the other side of the troll's torso and the torso crawled over to the troll's decapitated head.

"Give it a chance, Gurken," said Arthur. "You were quite excited about saving the goblin; perhaps the trolls are just as worthy a creature?"

Gurken huffed.

The goblin jumped up and down, though it obtained no more than an inch of difference between the two extremes. It was still vibrating its arms; it started to make some strange sounds. "MMMmmm Hmmm mmmmuuuuhhh."

"I think the goblin is trying to tell us something," Pellonia remarked. The goblin nodded to the best of its ability.

Arthur rubbed his chin. "Perhaps he knows where the orb is located. Gurken, get the drawing and show him." Gurken took off his pack and looked through it for the scroll.

"Ah se'en where da orb is," said a voice. Everyone turned toward the voice. The troll, completely healed, loomed over them. It was twice as tall as Arthur. Its mouth twisted into a vicious smile, six-inch fangs protruding from its mouth. "Ah take you der. You comin' wit me."

The troll reached a hand down and grabbed Pellonia, its hand wrapping around her head. It lifted her into the air and slammed her head down to the ground. She didn't get up.

Moog ran, the goblin fell over and rolled away, Arthur took a few steps back and pulled out his orb, and Gurken drew his axe, roared and charged the troll. Berkano, the dwarfen rune of feeling anxiety about someone close to you, glowed a fierce orange upon the axe's head.

The troll batted the axe aside and stabbed Gurken in the shoulder with one of its claws. The troll's hand sizzled and burned where it struck the axe, and the troll recoiled in pain. Gurken picked his shield from the ground and smashed it into the troll's leg. There were the sickening sounds of ligaments popping and tendons tearing as the troll fell to one knee, a smile upon its face.

Arthur said, "Intentoque lux trabem!" A pencil-thin beam of light shot from the orb, slicing into the troll. The troll continued to smile.

"Littl' light no hurt Blod, Blod too strong," said the troll.

"The little light doesn't hurt Blod," corrected Arthur. He dragged the beam across the troll's flesh, slicing through it easily, but the flesh mended and healed just as quickly.

Blod furrowed its brows, grinned wickedly. "Yes,

THE BERSERKER AND THE PEDANT

wizard. Littl' light no hurt Blod. But, Blod hurt you." Blod stood, the ligaments and tendons on his knee healing, slurping and popping back into place. Blod stepped on Gurken, slamming him to the ground as he strode over him. Blod reached out, and its fingers fell off, cut by Arthur's beam. Blod slashed Arthur across the neck with the claws of his other hand, slicing off Arthur's head.

Arthur fell to the ground, the orb bouncing out of his hand and rolling over to the bushes, where it came to rest. Moog peeked out of the bush, reached out and grabbed the orb.

Blod grabbed the sack that had held the goblins and tossed the unconscious bodies of Gurken, Pellonia and Arthur into it.

"Arthur die lots," Moog said. "Moog made quick resurrection spell." Moog stabbed at a glowing dot on the orb with his finger. A light shone down from the heavens, and Arthur started the process of growing from a speck again. The troll grabbed Moog and threw him in the sack. Then the troll saw Arthur growing and watched, curious. When Arthur had grown to full size, the troll looked at Arthur's corpse and back to Arthur again.

"Blod takes both," Blod said and threw Arthur and his corpse into the sack. Blod wandered over to the goblin, which had gotten stuck rolling up against a tree. He picked the goblin up, smelled it, wrinkled his nose and tossed it into the sack as well. Finally,

Blod closed the bag and wandered off to find the elves.

"Quit squirmin'," Blod said, smacking the sack. "Leon take Blod back. Blod finds you!"

Antic watched the troll lumber off. He'd been lazing around in Arthur's robes, luxuriating in the warmth of his companion, when he was jerked awake and flung out of the robes and into the forest. Antic skittered around the clearing, sniffing everything he could find. There was quite a bit of troll blood, dwarfen blood, and the scent of death where his companion had lain. Antic's antennae quivered, and he wandered away in the direction opposite the path the troll had taken.

Episode Twelve

THE BERSERKER AND THE AWAKENING

"What happened?" Arthur asked. "One second I'm being killed by goblins, the next I'm being thrown into a sack by a troll!"

Arthur, Gurken, Moog and the goblin were at the bottom of a tall muddy pit, the walls of which rose rather sharply, and had no obvious ways to climb out. After walking for a while, the troll had removed Pellonia from the sack, overturned it, and dumped everyone else into the pit. The goblin bounced around a few times and rolled to a stop while Arthur, Gurken and Moog landed with a loud splut.

"Don't you remember searching for Pellonia? Or rescuing the goblin and fighting the troll?" Gurken responded.

"Why would we rescue a goblin?" asked Arthur. "Didn't they just kill me?"

"Pellonia's right. You do hold a grudge for a long time," said Gurken.

"They killed me TWO hours ago!"

"It's been a couple of days," said Gurken. Moog nodded.

"Not to me, it hasn't! And why am I human again, and why is that" - Arthur pointed at his corpse - "human, and why is it here? Why do we have a goblin dressed up like a scarecrow on a feast day? Where is my centaur corpse?"

"Centaur corpses," corrected Moog. Arthur both scowled and looked hopelessly confused.

"Wizards ask too many questions," Gurken said, looking at Moog. Moog nodded.

Arthur leaned his head against his hands and said, "I don't think I'm being unreasonable."

Arthur stripped his corpse of wizarding robes and put them on. Patting his chest, hips, and arms, he asked, "Where's Antic?"

᛭

Pellonia woke up thinking, *I've been spending entirely too much time waking up.* She was lying on a cot. She cracked open her eyes and saw Melody in a chair to her left and Leon in a chair to her right. Leon had one arm draped over the back of the chair and was sitting cross-legged, while Melody was sitting with her hands in her lap. They were both staring at her.

"Oh, good!" Leon exclaimed. "She's awake! Well, let's get going." He hopped off the chair. Pellonia sat up on the cot, seeing that they were in a rather large tent, large enough that some might even consider it to be a small pavilion.

THE BERSERKER AND THE PEDANT

"Slow down, Leon," Melody said. "We don't even know yet if she wants to come with us."

"Pfffhhh. Of course she wants to come with us. Why wouldn't she? It's time for her first Awakening and the Phage is comin-"

"What's the Phage?" Pellonia asked.

Leon paused mid-sentence. "I can't tell you that, you aren't Awakened."

"So, let me see if I understand. If I want to know about the Phage, I have to be Awakened, and I should be Awakened because of the Phage?"

"That about covers it," said Leon. "Let's get going, our ship's leaving. The Phage will arrive soon."

"What about my friends?" Pellonia asked. "Can they come as well?"

"Absolutely not!" Leon gasped. "Chimarae are not permitted on board."

"What are chimerae? No, no, let me guess; you can't tell me that either?"

"Yeeaaahhh. No."

Melody said, "Leon, you aren't very good at not saying things you're not supposed to say, are you?"

"She is one of us, after all. It's a bit confusing."

"Why don't you go get the trolls, and I'll talk to Pellonia," Melody said.

"That sounds good to me." Leon walked out of the tent.

Melody watched Leon leave, waited a moment,

then said "The Phage are creatures from another world. We're at war with them, and they'll be coming to this world soon. Chimerae are creatures we've created to fight the Phage."

"Arthur, Gurken and Moog are chimerae?"

"Gurken and Moog are chimerae. Arthur is human."

"And humans aren't chimerae?"

"No, humans aren't chimerae."

Pellonia sat expressionless for a time, then looked at Melody with a look of determination. "It doesn't matter if the Phage are coming, I won't abandon my friends. If they stay, I'm staying too."

"Oomph," Arthur said. "How can you two be so short and yet weigh so much?" Moog was standing on Arthur's shoulders, and Gurken was standing on Moog's head, stretching up and pulling himself out of the pit.

Gurken stood up near the edge of the pit, pounded his chest with one hand and said, "Thick bones!" He reached his axe handle into the pit and pulled Moog out. Arthur tossed the goblin and the rest of their equipment up and over the edge of the pit, grabbed the axe hilt and walked up the side of the pit while Gurken and Moog pulled.

"Okay," said Arthur. "Here's the plan. First, we rescue Pellonia. Second, we locate and retrieve the orb. Third, we get out of here."

"That's more of a list of goals than it is a plan," Gurken objected.

"I'm afraid that I must agree," said a voice behind them. They turned and saw Leon, who they had yet to meet, standing with his arms crossed. Three trolls loomed over him, smiling and drooling. One was staring at the goblin, running his tongue over his lips.

Leon said, "That's not much of a plan. Plans are more specific. They're broken down into actual steps for accomplishing the goals. And besides, you can't have Pellonia. She's coming with us."

"An' ah'm gonna eat yur goblin. Taassstttyyyy," said the troll.

"Hush," said Leon, "You aren't helping."

Gurken drew his axe. "I don't know who you are, elf, but you will release Pellonia at once." Tiwaz, the dwarfen rune of knowing where one's true strengths lie, glowed a virulent amber, and upside down, on Gurken's axe.

Leon looked at the axe and then back to Gurken. "You're Durstin's boy, aren't you? I've heard of you. Honestly, I don't know what he was thinking. How are you going to save this world? You can't, you're just a dwarf with anger issu-" Leon ducked just fast enough to dodge the bulk of the blow, but the axe clipped the top of his head, knocking him to the ground. The trolls' eyes grew wide in shock. One pointed while covering its mouth and snickering.

Leon pulled himself up and saw the trolls laughing; his eyes turned the color of elven steel. Three orbs flew off his back and hovered a foot over his head, covered in ice, fire, and lightning. "Ignis!" shouted Leon, pointing at Gurken. A gout of flame erupted from an orb, sending a searing wall of flames toward Gurken.

Moog ran, rolling the goblin along in front of him. Arthur stepped back and drew his orb. The trolls lumbered towards him, bumping into each other in their haste. Arthur said "Lux, Lux, LUX!" and bright lights flashed in the trolls' eyes. The trolls howled in pain and rubbed at their eyes.

Algiz, the dwarfen rune of protection, glowed on Gurken's axe, and a protective dome formed over Gurken. The orb's fire harmlessly licked at the dome.

Leon swore an oath. "Durstin has outfit you well. Fortunately, I don't need these toys to deal with you." Leon drew his sword, the veins of his skin engorged and darkened into a sharp bluish-steel sheen, and then he was gone, moving so fast as to appear nothing more than a blur. Gurken's axe flew from his grip, his protective dome collapsing. Blood spurted from Gurken's shoulder, and his knee buckled and collapsed from blows too quick to observe.

Gurken fell to the ground; Leon stopped moving;

his sword's tip quivered, humming against Gurken's neck. "Do you yield, dwarf?" Leon asked, smirking.

The trolls finally adapted to the flashing lights in their eyes through the ingenious method known as squinting. They charged toward Arthur once more.

"Intentoque lux trabem!" the wizard cried in desperation. A searing finger-sized beam cut through the trolls, their bones and flesh healing as fast as Arthur cut. Arthur said, "Oh, no, not again!" He stabbed at the orb with one finger and tossed it over his shoulder into the pit. He managed to say, "I do so hope this works," before the trolls reached him.

"It's not your battle, Pellonia," Melody said. "The chimerae will fight off the Phage; they've done it before on other worlds. They'll do it here as well... most likely."

"Most likely!"

"Well, they don't always win. The Phage adapts, and so do we. Win some, lose some." Melody shrugged.

"I can't believe you're so callous, Melody. You didn't used to be."

"That was a long time ago, Pellonia."

"It's only been seven years since I saw you."

"Time passes differently where we're going, Pel. It seemed like a few years to you, but it was a thousand years for me. I've been away for a very long time."

Pellonia's mouth dropped open. "A thousand years! Dead goblins, that's a long time! If I go, will it be that long for me?"

"No, this is your first Awakening. A century will pass for you, and just five years on this world. It'll be my third Awakening; ten thousand years will pass for me. Leon's already been through the third Awakening, so he's going to be your mentor."

Pellonia wrinkled up her face. "Can't you do it, instead?"

"I'm afraid not, I can't mentor you and go through the third Awakening at the same time."

"Shouldn't Leon be going through the fourth Awakening?" Pellonia asked hopefully.

Melody was silent for a time, and Pellonia didn't interrupt. Finally, Melody said, "One hundred thousand years. Only the All Mother has done that. She's quite mad because of it. Even we have limits."

"So, you can see," Melody continued, "why Arthur and the chimarae can't come. They would wither away and die of old age even during the first Awakening. We don't age, so we can survive."

A low hum and orange glow started emanating from a small table in the middle of the room. Pellonia had been so distracted, she hadn't noticed it before, but there it sat - a cube composed of polished elven steel. The Orb of Skzd rose, floating up and off

THE BERSERKER AND THE PEDANT

the table. It was vibrating, and one of its sides flickered to life with the image of Leon shooting flames at Gurken.

"Oh, no," said Melody. "Wait right here, I'll be back!" Melody took off running out of the small pavilion.

Pellonia screamed as she witnessed the trolls ripping Arthur apart and Leon pressing his sword against Gurken's neck.

Episode Thirteen

THE BERSERKER AND THE ORB

Arthur woke up in a pit, naked. He spent some small amount of time considering what it meant that his corpse was lying next to him, naked and human.

The last thing, Arthur thought, *that I remember was Melody running off with Pellonia. I swore an oath to her parents to protect her, and to the best of my abilities, I have. But then I was killed by goblins. At least Pellonia is safe with her older sister. But why isn't my corpse a centaur, and why aren't we on a cliff?*

Arthur saw a glint of elven steel in the mud, reached out and picked up his orb. There was a loud splut next to him, splashing his face with mud. Arthur wiped the mud from his eyes and saw his decapitated head looking back at him.

That is decidedly odd, Arthur thought. *I should likely be scared or repulsed by this event, but seeing as my corpse is there, and I am here, and I have at least one more corpse lazing about somewhere, it is no tremendous shock that my head should come rolling around. I should, however, prepare to defend myself, in case whatever is causing me to die over and over again decides to come back.*

Arthur noted that the orb was already set to full power, so he tightened the lens until the beam was set to full intensity and pointed it up. Three trolls looked over the edge, grinning in anticipation. They jumped in the pit.

"Well, now, little dwarf," Leon said. "It appears Durstin's little creature isn't nearly as effective as Durstin bragged." Leon chuckled. "I'm quite sorry about your friend. It was not my intention for the trolls to eat him." Leon's eyes shone the color of elven steel, and his veins bulged the same color. He held his blade against Gurken's throat, pinning him to the ground. Gurken gripped the blade with both hands, blood running down his arms.

The blood rage came upon Gurken. His heart thumped louder and louder, drowning out the sounds of the mewling elf. His vision tinged with crimson as he was pulled into a berserker's trance. Gurken fought the pull harder than he'd ever fought it before, knowing that he tended not to make the best decisions while in a rage, and that good decisions needed to be made or he might never see Pellonia or Arthur again.

Pellonia was in the tent, but she was not about to wait for Melody to return. She walked over to the Orb of Skzd. It was a cube as big as her forearm on all sides and hovered just above a small table in the middle of the large tent. She stood on her toes and stretched out, touching the image of Gurken moving on its face. Her finger hit a smooth surface. It was like a painting that changed. She climbed onto the table and took the cube in both hands.

The cube stayed in place. She turned it and it spun like a top. There were raised circular bits on the top with elvish writing next to them. She didn't understand most of the writing; it was in elvish, but the words were unfamiliar. "Gee-oh-low-cate," Pellonia sounded out the word. She scratched her head. "I do so wish Arthur were here; he could figure this out. If only I knew where to find him."

Gurken roared. "I don't know who you are, elf, but I am Gurken Stonebiter, avatar of Durstin Firebeard, and I will NOT BE TRIFLED WITH." His muscles bulged, veins engorged with blood and he slowly, ever so slowly, moved the blade from his throat.

Leon's eyes opened wide, then squinted. He tried to push the blade down into Gurken's throat, but the blade still moved away. Beads of liquid metal sweat formed on his forehead, and the blade began to

THE BERSERKER AND THE PEDANT

move back towards Gurken's throat. Gurken rolled to the side and the blade bit into the ground an inch from his neck, shattering from the force of Leon's blow.

Gurken raised a hand and Raidho, the Dwarfen rune of seeing the right move for yourself and acting upon it, pulsed with a violet light on the blade of Gurken's axe. The axe flew from the ground and landed in Gurken's hands as he leapt into the air, Leon directly below him. Leon turned and saw the axe coming down on his head and then he was gone, moving so fast he wasn't even a blur.

Leon rained blow upon blow on Gurken, faster than Gurken could see or comprehend. Gurken was struck sixteen times before he felt the first blow, and it was as if a sack of bricks crushed his face. Gurken lay on the ground, groaning, a bloody pulp. Leon stood over Gurken, a steel-colored mist coming from his eyes, face twisted in rage.

"I rather liked that blade, dwarf." He spat the word. Gurken rolled onto his back and lifted one hand towards Leon.

"I'm going to enjoy this," Leon said, pulling back one hand into a fist and grabbing Gurken's jerkin with the other.

"Free-queen-see," read Pellonia. "Hmm... Attitude. I don't see how that can help. Power! We could certainly use some more of that!" Pellonia rubbed at the word and said, "Potestas!" Nothing happened. She rubbed the raised circular protrusion next to it; it depressed and made a clicking sound. Suddenly, the cube went dark and fell to the table.

"What kind of stupid 'power' is that?" Pellonia said.

Leon dropped Gurken and stumbled a step back. His eyes turned a shade of blue and his veins no longer bulged. "Gaaaah," he yelled, clutching the sides of his head. Gurken grinned and pulled himself to his feet. He walked over to his axe and, bending slightly, picked it up off the ground. "What's the matter, Leon? Did your magic abandon you?"

The three orbs flew off Leon's shoulders, orienting towards Gurken, but before they could act, Gurken planted his axe into Leon's head with a satisfying thunk. Dagaz, the dwarfen rune of completion and ending, glowed green on the axe's head. The orbs fell to the ground. Leon stumbled back, an empty expression on his face, the axe protruding from his head. Blood ran down his face, a mixture of crimson and elven steel. He fell to the ground and his eyes went white.

The three trolls landed in the bottom of the pit,

THE BERSERKER AND THE PEDANT

Arthur backed into a corner and held up the orb between them.

"Oho! A secon' helpin'. Ah didn't expect such a treat," said Blod.

"Oh, aye, we shood eat wizurds mo' often, and eat 'em slow," agreed Boan.

"Ahm gonna rip off 'is ahm quick and sup on 'is blud," proclaimed Maro.

"You're going to 'rip off his arm quickly'," said Arthur. "It's an adverb, not an adjective."

"Et's a flat adverb," said Maro, raising a finger. "Take et easy!"

Arthur squinted at Maro and pursed his lips. "Some may subscribe to the antiquated use of 'flat adverbs,' but I most certainly do NOT! Intentoque lux trabem!"

The light from the pit poured into the orb, leaving them momentarily shrouded in darkness. A waterfall of light streamed into the pit from above. The orb began to glow a bright yellow and the trolls cackled with laughter.

"Nawt dis agen," Blod said, rolling his eyes as a beam sprouted from the orb, cutting into his arm. He shrieked as the arm fell off. Elven steel-colored blood leaked from the wound, before the stump healed over. "Oh, no," Blod said. "Dat's a problem." Arthur twirled the beam around Blod's body, which fell into pieces.

Boan and Maro tried to scramble up the side of

the pit, but were quickly fricasseed - that is, they were sliced into small pieces and cooked in their own juices. The beam shut off and light returned to the small pit.

"Well, I believe that is the end of those horrid creatures. Flat adverbs, indeed."

Melody rounded the corner, yelling, "Leon! Don't hurt them, they'r- Oh!" Gurken pulled his axe out of Leon's head, spattering bits of steel gray ichor over the ground. He smiled at Melody.

"Milady," Gurken said, touching the axe to his head.

"You... you... you killed Leon? But... how?"

"With an axe," Gurken said matter-of-factly, holding his axe in the air.

"But... he's... he's so fast."

"Nothing a well-timed axe can't handle."

Melody blinked at Gurken, then walked over to Leon. She crouched over Leon and picked up one of his orbs from the ground. She fiddled with the orb a bit, then pointed it at Leon. A red line appeared at the tip of his head, then moved down his body. A jarring "ehhh-ehhhh" emanated from the orb. Melody sighed.

She put a hand to her head. "He's not going to remember any of this. He wasn't scanned since before he came down here." After a moment, she

THE BERSERKER AND THE PEDANT

pushed at the orb again and passed the red line over herself.

"Hullo up there!" Arthur's voice rose out of the pit. "Could I trouble anyone for a spot of help?"

Gurken walked to the edge of the cliff and looked down. Arthur was dangling from the orb, which was hovering a few feet below the top of the pit. His feet were spinning, trying to gain purchase on the walls. Gurken reached his axe down, handle first. Arthur grabbed it with one hand and Gurken pulled Arthur and the orb out of the pit.

Arthur saw Melody and blushed fiercely. He tried to cover himself, but the closest he could come was to hold the orb in front of him. He sidestepped over to a bloody patch on the ground where some rags remained of his clothes. They were torn to shreds.

"Take Leon's clothes," Melody suggested. "He won't be needing them." She did not smile.

Relieved, Arthur trotted over to Leon and changed into his clothes. Once he was changed, he turned to Melody and asked, "Where's Pellonia?"

Pellonia came around the bend with a sack draped over her shoulder. She saw Arthur, dropped the sack, and ran over to give him a big hug. She waved Gurken over, and the dwarf ambled over and the three of them squeezed each other tightly. Moog burst out of the bushes and ran over, hugging Melody's leg.

"I got it," Pellonia said. "I got the Orb of Skzd."

"Well done, Pellonia," said Arthur.
"Well done," Gurken agreed.
"Mooooog," said Moog.

Episode Fourteen

THE BERSERKER AND THE CAVE

"I'm afraid I can't let you keep the Orb of Skzd," Melody said. "I need it."

Gurken, Arthur, Pellonia and Moog broke from their group hug. Pellonia pressed her eyebrows together, looking irritated and thoughtful all at once. Arthur looked at Melody, his fingers running over his orb, clicking a piece back and forth. Moog shrugged. Gurken, well...

"You can't have it," said Gurken.

"I'm sorry that I didn't tell you about it sooner, but... look, this probably sounds ridiculous to you, but the fate of the world depends on my taking that cube."

Gurken furled his eyebrows and shifted his jaw from side to side. Melody was ten feet away; the cube lay in the sack that Pellonia had dropped between them. Fehu, the dwarfen rune of possessions won or earned, seared into the head of Gurken's axe, burning like coals in a dying fire.

"You cannot have it," Gurken said, matter-of-factly.

Melody hesitated, then took a step towards the sack. Gurken growled, raising the axe and leaning towards her. Pellonia started to move, but Melody stopped and retreated a step.

"Enough! Enough, elf-slayer. The cube is yours." She crossed her arms while Gurken, Arthur, Pellonia and Moog walked over to the sack. Pellonia opened the sack, revealing a polished cube of gleaming elven steel about a foot on each side.

"It's bigger than I thought it would be," said Arthur.

"I don't understand why you're surprised, wizard. It's exactly the size it is on the scroll. I thought wizards paid attention to such details," Gurken said.

Arthur pursed his lips.

Moog gingerly reached out, his finger getting closer and closer. When it touched, he jumped behind Arthur, peeking out from between his legs. Nothing happened. Gurken knocked on it with a fist. Still, nothing happened.

Pellonia said, "I think I broke it. It showed you were fighting, so when Melody left, I tried to make it give you more power, but then it just died. Maybe you're already too powerful?"

Melody smiled. "I-," she began.

"Silence, elf!" Gurken said. She stopped smiling.

"You know," said Pellonia. "I'm an elf as well. You don't need to say it with such a sneer in your voice."

"Right. Sorry." Gurken turned back to Melody. "Silence, woman!" Pellonia crossed her arms and glared. Gurken withered under her stare.

"What?" Gurken said. "What should I say?"

"How about something that doesn't insult my race or my gender?" said Pellonia.

Gurken looked apologetic, then turned back to Melody and glared. "Silence, vanquished one!" He looked at Pellonia without turning his head. She nodded. They all looked back at the cube.

"Let me try," Arthur said.

He waved a hand over the cube, and a layer of metal on top turned to liquid and drained into the cube, leaving behind circular metal protrusions and words. Arthur depressed the circular protrusion next to the word "Power." The cube lifted a foot into the air. It hummed and glowed a faint blue from one side as indecipherable words formed at the bottom and moved up the side, disappearing when they reached the top of the cube.

"Woah," Pellonia said. "Now what?"

"I haven't the foggiest," Arthur said. "Given enough time, I'm sure I could figure out what it does."

Melody raised her hand in the air and waved it around. Gurken watched her and raised an eyebrow.

"I think she wants to say something," Pellonia said.

"Go ahead," said Gurken, flipping his hand open in her direction, "You may speak."

"Thank you. Look, the Orb of Skzd is yours, I won't take it. I promise. But we really need to decide what to do next. The Phage will be here soon, and Leon was a pivotal part of the plan to save this world."

"Why don't we resurrect him?" asked Pellonia.

"He hasn't been scanned since we arrived, so he won't remember anything that's happened. He won't be much help."

"What is this 'scan' of which you speak?" Arthur asked.

"We use an orb to scan your body, and it remembers you exactly as you were when you were last scanned. Then, when you're resurrected, a perfect copy is made. If there's no scan, that's fine as long as your body is more-or-less intact. Leon... well... His head is in no condition..." She trailed off.

Arthur's eyes opened wide. He took out his smaller orb of light and fiddled with it; a red horizontal beam shot out, and he ran it up and down his body. Then he did the same for Pellonia, Gurken and Moog. Gurken rolled the goblin over and after a few moments of intense staring back and forth, Arthur did the goblin too. "Does anyone know where Antic is?" Arthur asked. Everyone shook their head. Arthur sighed and put the orb away.

"Now that that's over," Gurken said. "What was

that bit about saving the world?"

"I almost wish I were a centaur again," Arthur said. Gurken, Pellonia, Melody, Arthur, Moog and the goblin stood at the entrance to a cave in the side of a particularly large mountain. A rather rickety fence encircled the opening. After Melody had explained about the invading Phage, they'd followed an elven path through the forest, walking for several days before arriving.

"Do you know what's better for extended walks?" Arthur asked. "Hooves. Hooves are far superior for walking compared to feet."

Moog raised an eyebrow at Arthur as if to say, "I can arrange that."

Arthur shook his head.

"Very well, Melody," said Gurken. "We've trusted you this far. Why are we here?"

"Leon had been working on getting all of the goblin tribes together to help fight the invasion."

Gurken furled his brows. "Voluntarily, I'm sure," he said.

"Well... no, not exactly. We've been collecting them for several months and containing them in this cave. Goblins are very afraid of trolls; we were going to use the trolls to herd the goblins through a portal opened by the Orb of Skzd and towards the invaders, but I'm afraid we can't do that now. Maybe if Arthur and I take the orbs, we can herd th-"

"We're not herding anyone," Gurken said.

"But the fa-"

"I know, the fate of the world," said Gurken.

"But, without the goblins this wor-"

"I'm afraid that I must agree with Gurken," Arthur interjected. "A slave army, besides being entirely ineffective, is utterly immoral."

"I'm with Gurken as well," said Pellonia, hands on her hips.

"Moog like Gurken better," said Moog.

"You want to give up and let the Phage kill everyone and take over the world?" Melody said, voice rising in pitch as she spoke.

"No," said Gurken. "That's not acceptable, either."

"What then?"

"We ask them," Gurken said.

"Ask them? Ask the Phage to go away, won't they please? They're invading, Gurken. I don't think asking them politely to please go away will accomplish anything."

"Ask the goblins," Gurken said.

"Ah. That does make more sense. Still, there are thousands of them; how do we ask them all? Send around a petition? They can't read!"

"The same way you'd ask for the help of any people. You ask their leaders."

"They have leaders?"

THE BERSERKER AND THE PEDANT

"You don't know much about goblins, do you?"

"Well, no, just enough to know they will be useful against the Phage."

Arthur interjected again, "I don't see how they'll be of any use in battle, anyway. They'll probably die just trying to get to the battlefield."

Gurken ignored Arthur and continued, "Tell me where you want the goblins to go, and we'll meet you there."

Gurken entered the cave, holding a torch in one hand and his axe slung on his back. He walked for a time, twisting through the dank tunnels, but found nothing. From time to time, he heard chattering in the distance, but never saw anything. He walked for several hours and finally came upon a small goblin standing in the middle of the tunnel, holding a spear.

"HALT!" said the goblin, pointing the spear toward Gurken. Gurken halted.

"Hail, fierce goblin warrior. It is I, Gurken Stonebiter. I'm on a quest to find the leaders of the goblin clans. May I, perhaps, speak to your Gr-ma?"

The goblin eyed Gurken suspiciously, but perhaps due to Gurken's friendly demeanor, didn't immediately attack. "Do you have a pass?" asked the goblin.

"Pardon, a pass?"

"Yes. You have it exactly. You need a pass to travel in Gr-ma's tunnel."

Gurken felt his berserker rage roil inside of him. Here was yet another pass-seeking fool. He reached behind him, touching the hilt of his axe. The goblin whistled, and two more goblins sprang out of the shadows, standing on either side of the first goblin. "Come on, then," the goblin said, hopping from side to side. "Have at you!" The goblin on the left eyed Gurken suspiciously; the one on the right picked his nose.

Gurken fought down his rage. He needed the goblins' help. When the heat inside of him had cooled to a controllable level, he raised his hands in surrender and smiled. Then, he lowered one hand to his beard and lifted up the cord of knots Gr-ma had tied. The goblins eyes grew wide. "Here's my pass," Gurken said. The goblin approached tentatively, reaching up to touch the cord. He rubbed a knot with his fingers, then leapt back.

"It's a cord with knots in it, so what? Anyone could hav-" Gurken sung one of the songs Gr-ma had taught him. It was a low, sad song about the quick, violent life of a goblin and the hope for a better, simpler and longer life filled with good food and a happy, healthy family. The three goblins stood transfixed by what they heard, tears running down their face.

When he stopped, the first goblin wiped his face

THE BERSERKER AND THE PEDANT

and said, "Come with us, lore keeper. We'll take you to Gr-ma's den." The third goblin stopped digging in his nose, and turned a bit too quickly, impaling himself on the the first goblin's spear. He slumped over, dead. The first goblin shook him off the spear, turned and walked down the tunnel, gesturing for Gurken to follow.

Episode Fifteen

THE BERSERKER AND THE WALNUT

Melody stood on the edge of a cliff, overlooking a vast valley. It was midday and the sun burned hotly overhead. There wasn't a cloud to be seen. They had gone on a four-day hike up and around the mountain from where they had left Gurken. The valley stretched on for miles in front of her.

Melody was looking at the village from which Gurken and Pellonia had started their quest, the hill where Moog lived, and another small mountain. Actually, it was a large ant hill - that is, a small hill made from the activities of large ants, not a large hill made by the activity of small ants, though perhaps the two would be difficult to distinguish.

Pellonia walked up to her sister. "Here?" she asked, panting for breath in the thinner air.

"Here," Melody agreed, putting her arm around Pellonia's neck and pulling her in close. They stayed like that for a moment.

Arthur finally caught up, weighed down by a backpack. Within which were four orbs and The

THE BERSERKER AND THE PEDANT

Orb. He also carried the goblin under one arm. He set the goblin down, dropped the pack to the ground and staggered, sitting down to avoid falling. "Finally!" he said. "I'm not a pack animal, you know. I can't keep up this march any longer."

Melody walked over and pulled one of the smaller orbs from the backpack, Arthur was too tired to resist. She fiddled with the orb and a layer of frost formed over its exterior. She set it just above Arthur's head and let go. It floated, lightly dusting Arthur with snow. Arthur wrinkled his eyebrows. "Ah... I see that it floats. By itself. Nice of you to wait until now to show me," he said. "I suppose that all of the orbs can float?" Melody smiled.

She pulled out the other small orbs and showed Arthur how to make them float. There were now four small orbs floating about a foot over Arthur's head, slowly rotating and moving around in a circle. "It would be best if you learned how to use those," Melody said. "Moog, you too."

Moog trotted over to Arthur, and they started fiddling with the orbs and speaking on mysticism and the nature of magic.

Melody took the Orb of Skzd out of the sack, waved her hand over it, and pushed her finger on a protrusion on top. The Orb began floating. She pushed the Orb of Skzd near the edge of the cliff, stopping it about two feet from the edge.

"What are you doing?" Pellonia asked.

"The Phage will be here soon. I need to prepare."

Melody pushed another protrusion and the side closest to her fell open, coming to rest horizontally. On top of it were rows of protrusions with elven letters, numbers and other symbols engraved on them. A roughly rectangular transparent image formed behind the Orb, a dark blue shape about the size of a small house. Through the image, the valley and sky were visible.

Melody wiggled her fingers over the protrusions, and a crimson dot appeared on the image in the sky. Pellonia walked to the edge of the rectangle and looked behind the image; the red dot was gone. She looked back to the image and the dot was still there. Numerous lines and numbers started appearing in the image. The lines extended from the dot and ran to a point in the valley several hours hike in front of them, followed by another line moving towards them. The numbers were constantly changing.

"What's that?" Pellonia asked, pointing at the red dot.

"That," Melody said, not looking up from the Orb, "is the Phage, and that" - she pointed at the lines - "is their trajectory, the path they're coming in on."

Pellonia squinted, "Where are they flying from?" She looked around the side of the image again, and the lines and numbers were gone. She looked through the image and they were back again.

THE BERSERKER AND THE PEDANT

"Another world," Melody said. "I don't know which one."

"An odd way to arrive. I'd have thought they'd use some sort of mystic portal."

Melody glanced at Pellonia, then went back to working on the Orb. "All of this is explained during the Awakening, Pellonia."

"Oh," Pellonia said and fell silent.

Melody pushed a protrusion on the orb and a beam of light projected onto the ground, forming into an upright disc of light. Through the disc, Pellonia could see a clearing in the forest.

"Come on, Gurken, where are you?" Melody said. She stabbed the protrusion on the Orb with her finger, and the disc collapsed and faded away.

The image on the rectangle in front of the valley blurred and changed, then Gurken's face stared back at them. Well, almost Gurken's face. It looked like Gurken, but he was - well - clean-shaven and his hair was combed. He didn't have any scars and was dressed in a strange blue outfit that clung to his skin. Also, his ears were pointed.

"Melody!" strange Gurken said. "Thank God! I'd begun to think the worst. Where's Leon? We need the goblins; everyone else is in place."

"Durstin," Melody said. Pellonia's eyes widened at the mention of the dwarfen god of butchery and battle's name. Melody continued, "Good to see you again. Time is short, so I'll be brief. I'm fine. Leon's dead. He had an... altercation with Gurken. The trolls are dead too, so Gurken is fetching the goblins."

"Ha! Leon won't ever live this down." Then Durstin's face grew serious. "Are we done then? Do we pull out?"

"Abandon this world to the Phage? No," Melody said, looking over at Pellonia. "I think we can still pull it off - if - the dwarf can bring the goblins."

"He can do it," Pellonia said, nodding.

"Is that little Pellonia?" Durstin asked. "Why, it's been ages since I last saw you. You're almost all grown up. I can't wait to see you on board the ship and hear all about your adventures."

The red light reappeared on the image, flashing above Durstin's head. It was no longer a small speck, it was as big as an egg. Pellonia looked around the image and saw a dark object far off in the distance.

"Melody, the dwarves are in position, but they'll be slaughtered without the goblins. The goblins must strike first," Durstin said.

"I understand. I'll do my best, but this was Leon's plan. I was just supposed to watch. I'm a bit overwhelmed, to be honest."

Pellonia's jaw dropped. Melody, overwhelmed?

"You'll do fine. Now, I've got to go finish my own preparations. I'll see you back on board the ship." With that, Durstin's face faded from view, and the lines and numbers returned. The glowing red dot

THE BERSERKER AND THE PEDANT

was now the size of a fist and growing.

Melody stopped playing with the Orb and turned to Pellonia.

"I'm sorry I have to do this, but it's time to decide. We may need to leave very quickly and I won't have time to ask once the battle starts. What's it going to be? Stay here and remain a little girl, or come with us, undergo the Awakening and become a woman?"

Pellonia's eyes grew wide. "I - uh - don't know."

"I'm sorry, you have to choose and you have to choose now. I can't decide this for you, it's a decision you have to come to on your own."

Pellonia blinked rapidly and sniffed. "I... I'm sorry, I don't know... I can't, I just can't." She turned and ran down the mountain.

Melody ran after her, "Pellonia, wait!"

An ear-piercing boom thundered over the valley. Everyone looked. The ball was now the size of a warrior's shield, traveling high in the air toward them. Flames engulfed it as they watched, and it grew larger and larger as it came closer.

Pellonia kept on running. Melody turned to Arthur and yelled over the roaring of the fireball. "Go and get her!" Arthur ran down the mountain after Pellonia, orbs whizzing about his head. Moog jogged after them both. Melody ran back to the Orb of Skzd. The ball of fire in the air now took up a sizable portion of the sky.

Arthur ran after Pellonia down the mountain, stepping over rocks and roots. Pellonia was quick, but Arthur and Moog managed to keep pace. Pellonia turned and slid down a steep slope. Arthur followed without hesitation. Pellonia slid on her feet while Arthur and Moog tumbled head over heels. In a few moments, they were at the bottom. Pellonia ran off into the trees, while Arthur and Moog lay there, recovering from the fall.

Arthur stood up and pulled Moog to his feet. They walked in the direction Pellonia had gone. After a time, Arthur heard her sobbing and followed the sound until he found her. She was sitting, leaning with her back against a tree, knees bent with her arms around them. Her head was against her legs, and she was rocking.

Arthur sat down next to her and put an arm around her. Moog studied some branches off to the side. Arthur didn't say anything. The orbs circled over his head. Pellonia leaned into Arthur and cried. Eventually, she tapered off and sniffled.

"I don't want to go, Arthur," she said. "But I think I should."

Arthur nodded. "I think that you should, as well. I'll be here, Pellonia. You can always come back later."

"Everything will be different, Arthur. Melody

told me we'd be back in five years, but a century will have passed for me. I don't want to be away from you for that long. Or from Gurken, or even Moog. I love it here. I... I'm happy you're here."

"I'm happy you're here, too." Arthur said. They sat for a time, holding each other. Finally, Arthur said, "There might be a way for you to stay with us and undergo the Awakening."

Melody watched as the ball of fire flew into the valley, thick, roiling waves of black smoke streaming behind. It hurled toward the surface at enormous speed. The mountain rumbled and shook as the fireball collided with the ground, gouging an enormous trail, miles long. Dirt flew hundreds of feet into the air, piling into a small mountain range in front of it.

The fire puffed out as it came to rest less than a mile in front of them. Melody could feel the heat from it wash over her. It had the appearance of a blackened walnut, as big as the mountain on which they stood. Smoke streamed off the blackened surface and dust billowed into the air, pooling around its top and spreading outwards, obscuring the sun.

"The Phage have arrived," Melody said.

Episode Sixteen

THE BERSERKER AND THE ELVES

"Are you sure you want to do this? It's irreversible. Once we do it, there's no going back," Arthur said.

"I'm sure," Pellonia said, nodding.

Arthur faced Pellonia. They stood in the forest, surrounded by tall pine trees. Moog stood next to Arthur, watching with a curious look on his face. Arthur took the orb of light and fiddled with it, then pointed it at Pellonia. A red horizontal beam shot out and ran up and down her.

"Very well," Arthur said. He pointed at Pellonia and said, "You've decided to stay with us, so you..." Arthur looked two feet to Pellonia's right and stabbed a finger at the orb, then pointed at the empty spot. Three beams of light shot out of the orb, connecting with the other orbs revolving around his head. Arthur's eyes opened wide and four beams of light descended from the heavens, each with a speck in the middle that grew from a fetus to adulthood.

"... you will go on the Awakening," Arthur finished feebly, dropping his hand. "Oh, no."

THE BERSERKER AND THE PEDANT

Five Pellonias put their hands on their hips and cocked their head to one side. "Hey! What did you just do?" they said in unison. "You were only supposed to make one more of me. Hey, stop saying what I'm saying. No, you stop it. Ugh." Pellonia glared at herself... herselves... theirselves?

"I... uh, clearly the orbs interacted in a way I didn't anticipate... yes." Arthur bit his lip while tapping on the orb of light with a finger.

Moog smiled. "Moog can mend." Moog picked up a sizable rock.

"No, no, Moog, that's not necessary. I don't believe your services will be required," Arthur said. Moog shrugged, dropping the rock.

Melody watched as the enormous Phage ship trembled. The sound of hard, heavy blows echoed through the valley. A crack formed in the top of the ship, accompanied by the sound of thunder. An enormous spike on the end of a huge tentacle punched through the surface of the ship. It was covered in circular folds of flesh that sucked at the air. The tentacle shot up hundreds of feet, whipping around violently.

"Keep it together," Melody said aloud. She'd been told to expect the unexpected, but this was beyond anything for which she was prepared. This thing shouldn't - couldn't - exist. It shouldn't be possible, yet there it was, plain to see. The mind is, under most circumstances, capable of making sense of the world, to compare what it now experiences to things it's experienced in the past. But how could the mind compare this? How could it make sense of the horror before her? It wasn't the tendril of an octopus that writhed and twisted in the valley before her, but that is all her mind could comprehend, so that is what she saw.

The tentacle exploded into countless small pieces that each moved on their own. Tiny creatures fell to the ground. They were small, visible only because there were so many of them. Melody held both hands up to the rectangular image in front of her and pulled her hands quickly apart. The image of the ship got bigger until she could no longer see all of it, then it centered on the hole and continued to get closer until the creatures were clearly visible.

Each creature was a mass of tentacles, balled up and rolling, spreading out in all directions.

"I'm not going on the Awakening. I'm staying with Arthur," said Pellonia.

"You can't make me go. You said she would go," said Pellonia.

"I've already said that I'm staying. I'm the original. That was decided before any of you were even here," said Pellonia.

THE BERSERKER AND THE PEDANT

"You can't trick me. I said that I - that you - were going!" said Pellonia.

"Well, you all figure out who is going. I'm staying," said Pellonia.

The Pellonias had all dug into her... their... into Pellonia's pack, and fought over which particular outfit each was going to wear. Pellonia was quite happy, because she happened to be wearing her favorite outfit already. Besides, she had the only pair of shoes. Pellonia was happy because she'd been closest to the pack and obtained a clean set of travel gear and some slippers. Pellonia was upset because she'd only managed to obtain the backup outfit, to be worn in case the others became soiled. Pellonia was very upset because she'd been left with only soiled, wrinkled clothing from which to choose. Pellonia was furious, all she had was a sleep sack to hold around her.

Arthur threw up his hands. "I'm afraid that I'm at a loss. The five of you are going to have to decide what to do."

The Pellonias glared at each other. Simultaneously, they pointed at the Pellonia on their left and said, "You. You're going to the Awakening. Ugh." They all crossed their arms in disgust.

There was a terrible screeching from deep in the forest, then another, closer. The Pellonias looked at each other nervously, remembering their world was about to be invaded. There was movement in the trees, shadows darting too quick to make out. The Pellonias ran behind Arthur, huddling against each other and looking into the forest. Arthur plucked one of the small orbs from the air and handed it to Moog. The other three orbs stopped spinning around his head and oriented towards the things coming toward them.

The forest cast a great many shadows for the creatures to hide within, so they approached while seen only at the edges of perception, scurrying through the forest as fast as a man could run. One leapt from the trees, tentacles spread and erect as it leapt for Arthur's head. A beam of frost shot from one of the orbs, freezing the creature in a solid chunk of ice. It fell to the ground and shattered.

Two more leapt at them, one freezing and shattering as before, another engulfed in a torrent of flame from a second orb. It burned, withered and died.

Moog shot another with a bolt of lightning from the orb he'd been handed. Then the forest was alight with bolts, rays, torrents and beams. The air was thick with color. Orange silhouettes danced along the mountainside. Blue flashes flickered through the forest with epileptic fits. The sky grew dark, sunlight flowing into the orb of light. The repulsive scent of fried flesh filled the air. They kept coming, their numbers multiplying. They started to dodge the incoming blasts, some even resisted multiple shots,

THE BERSERKER AND THE PEDANT

absorbing the ice but burning by fire, ignoring the flames but pierced by light.

The Pellonias scrambled up the side of the mountain. Arthur turned and watched them run. They were too slow; they would never make it up the mountain before being overrun. Flashes of color thrummed behind him, hot pink tentacles writhed and squirmed and died. Arthur snatched the orb of ice from the air, pointing it at a spot between him and the Pellonias and said, "Obice glaciem." A blue-tinged beam shot from the orb, striking the ground and spreading horizontally in either direction. Huge spears of ice splintered out of the ground, rising thirty feet into the air and closing off the path between them.

A pink tentacle wrapped around Arthur's head, greedily sucking at his flesh. Five more tentacles wrapped around his face and head, leaving only one eye uncovered. The eye wrinkled and stretched wide in horror, as if the eye itself were screaming. Arthur tried to shout, but a tentacle slid into his open mouth. The creature began to pulse and its flesh writhed as Arthur clawed and bit at it, desperately trying to pull it off.

"Kill them," Arthur heard. He strained his uncovered eye, looking around for the source of the voice. It was a malevolent sound. An evil sound. Terror dripped off the words.

"Kill 'em all," the voice said again.

Arthur realized he had never before known fear. He realized it wasn't him speaking and yet, somehow, it was his voice.

Then, Arthur stopped. He stood still. The tentacles slid off his face with slurp-pop, slurp-pop sucking sounds and the creature half-slid, half-fell to the ground. Arthur's blue eyes gazed off into the distance, then turned green. Arthur slowly grinned, then he laughed, the evil, maniacal sounding laugh of a madman. His tongue had been replaced by a tentacle, writhing in his open mouth. He turned, plucking the orb of light out of the air, pointing it toward Moog and saying, his voice gravelly, hoarse and low, "Intentoque lux trabem!"

The world dimmed. The orbs of fire and ice fell to the ground, dark. Light from all around bent and twisted into the orb of light, which began to glow with white-hot intensity. Moog turned towards Arthur. Moog had the mournful, shamed look of a puppy whose master had been unfailingly kind but had suddenly, and without reason, struck him. In a quiet, squeaky voice, he said, "Moog?"

A beam the thickness of a spider's thread and bright as a reflection of the noonday sun shot from the orb for a fraction of a fraction of a moment. A tiny hole, insignificant in size but grand in import, seared into Moog's head. A wisp of smoke curled into the air. Moog fell to the ground, dead.

The tentacled creatures swarmed around Arthur,

THE BERSERKER AND THE PEDANT

staying a foot from him. The ground was a writhing pink blanket. Arthur picked the fallen orbs of fire and ice off the ground, fiddled with them, and sent them spinning around his head again. He walked over to Moog, the blanket undulating out of his way as he walked. He picked up the orb of lightning next to Moog's corpse and set it spinning over his head next to the others. Then Arthur fiddled with the orb of light.

On the surface of the orb was the image of Moog with the words "Delete backup? Yes. No."

"Yes," Arthur said, "The enemies of the Phage shall not rise again." The picture of Moog faded and vanished. A picture of Gurken faded into view. "Yes," said Arthur.

Melody. "Yes."

Arthur. "Yes."

Pellonia. "Yes."

Pellonia's face faded. Arthur set the orb to spinning around his head and walked away. As if following some unspoken command, the hot, moist blanket of pink creatures slithered under him, lifting him off the ground and carrying him, still standing, toward the alien ship.

"Where are those goblins?" Durstin bellowed. "Dwarves are dying in droves!"

"I-I don't know," Melody said.

"That's it, we're done. I'm calling a full retreat and pulling out. Even if they show up now, it's too late. If you're smart, you'll get to the ship now too," said Durstin. His image faded.

"Pellonia," Melody whispered, looking the way Pellonia had run. "Come on, where are you?"

A tentacle reached over the cliff and stuck to the ground. The tentacle was covered in a thick, viscous liquid. The creature pulled itself up over the cliff, just feet from Melody. Melody stabbed at the Orb and a glimmering dome formed over her. The creature leapt at her and dissolved when it hit the barrier. Two more pulled themselves up and leapt. The first struck and sizzled like eggs in hot oil, sliding down the barrier. The second stuck and walked on top of the dome, looking for an entrance. Small wisps of smoke rose from its feet. More creatures came over the cliff and swarmed towards her.

"Melody!" Pellonia shouted, running over the hill.

Melody stuck her hand in the air, palm towards Pellonia. "Wait!" she shouted. Pellonia didn't hear her and ran straight for the barrier. Melody's eyes grew wide with panic. She stabbed quickly at the orb and two beams of light descended from the heavens over her and Pellonia. The barrier dropped and Melody and Pellonia rose into the air.

The creatures leapt towards Melody, tentacles

THE BERSERKER AND THE PEDANT

outstretched, straining to latch onto an arm, a leg, anything. They missed, falling to the ground. More creatures piled on top of one another, followed by swarms of others, forming an enormous pyramid of writhing, sticky pink flesh. The topmost creature sprung skyward, straining to reach Melody. Melody curled into a fetal position as she flung skyward, trying to pull herself out of its reach, but the creature latched one tentacle onto her shoe and pulled itself up. Melody and the creature flew out of sight.

Pellonia looked down and saw herselves fleeing the tentacled creatures, then she, too, was pulled away and could see no more.

Episode Seventeen

The Berserker and the Pedant

Pellonia came up the side of the cliff in time to watch as Melody and Pellonia rose into the heavens on a beam of light.

Farewell Pellonia, thought Pellonia.

The other three Pellonias walked up beside her, out of breath from the hike, and looked up, watching her rise away. They heard an ominous slurp-pop, slurp-pop and looked to see a pink tentacled thing falling off the head of their stuffed goblin. The goblin's eyes turned green and it bared it's teeth in an evil grin and waddled towards them, cackling as it came.

The goblin lost it's footing. It tripped and the Pellonias watched as it rolled down the hill, picking up speed as it went, bumping over rocks and flying off the cliff.

Another dozen tiny pink tentacled things swarmed toward them. Pellonia screamed and ran. The other Pellonias watched her run and decided that Pellonia was most decidedly correct, and ran away as well. They split up, running in different

THE BERSERKER AND THE PEDANT

directions.

Pellonia ran down the hill and into a swarm of tentacles slurp-popping their way up. Surrounded, she curled into a ball and covered her head with her hands. The tentacled forms swarmed over her, clutching and pulling at her limbs until they managed to force them apart. One latched onto her head.

Pellonia ran to the cliff face and climbed down. She found a small outcropping of rocks on which to rest. A tentacled creature fell on her head from above.

Pellonia ran along the cliff, hoping to run through the creatures, which immediately grabbed her, pulled her down and latched on to her head.

Pellonia ran to the Orb of Skzd, pursued by six writhing tentacles lunging ever closer. She reached the Orb, frantically pushing at the protrusions with words next to them. The tentacled creatures slowed and crawled toward her, as if to prolong and savor the moment. Five of the creatures formed a ring around her and the sixth moved in.

As Pellonia stabbed at the Orb of Skzd, it projected a disc of light between her and the creatures. An axe swung through the portal and cleaved one of the tentacled creatures in two. Sowilo, the dwarfen rune of success, goals achieved and honor, blazed upon the axe's head. The creature burst into flames and screamed as it writhed and shriveled.

"Greetings, Pellonia," Gurken said, stepping through the disc and heaving the axe over one shoulder. "My apologies for being late. Goblins are exceedingly poor marchers. It was slow work to get them there."

Goblins swarmed through the portal and attacked. They stabbed at the tentacles with spears, missing as the creatures leapt upon their heads, latching onto the goblins' faces. Five goblins' eyes turned green as the tentacled creatures fell off, slurp-pop, slurp-pop. The goblins cackled, exposing their pointed teeth and a tentacle twisting where their tongue once lay.

One of the green-eyed goblins slipped and hit it's head on a rock. It died. The goblins, both those controlled by the creatures and those free from their control, watched him fall. They turned on each other and wrestled. Goblins died so quickly, it was difficult to keep track of which was controlled and which was not. In a moment's time, ten goblins and five tentacled corpses lay on the hillside.

Gurken surveyed the battle in valley from the side of the cliff, next to the Orb of Skzd.

"Pellonia, I think it time you took the orb and returned to the temple."

"I'd like to stay with you."

THE BERSERKER AND THE PEDANT

"We must complete our quest. I will follow after the battle."

Pellonia nodded. She wrapped Gurken in an enormous hug and said farewell. She put a hand over the orb and pressed a few of the protrusions. A portal opened with some rather startled priests standing on the other end. Pellonia pushed the Orb through to the temple and the portal closed behind her.

Gurken turned back to the valley. The fleshy pink creatures swarmed as far as he could see, their tentacles wrapping around anything that moved. Gurken turned and looked at the two dozen goblin leaders, clad in fur and feathers, assembled before him, standing in a neat row and waiting for his command. Behind them, tens, if not hundreds of thousands, of goblins formed a chaotic bumpy red blanket over the mountain.

One of the goblins' leaders, a Gr-ma named La, stepped forward. "Now?" she asked.

"Now," Gurken answered.

La turned and let loose a battle cry, a howling cackle that echoed down the mountain. The other leaders turned and shouted hoots and caws and growls. Everything grew silent, the wind howled, leaves rustled, a cricket buzzed, then the mountain erupted in a roar and the ground trembled as goblins screamed and charged down the mountain.

Gurken was covered in pink slime. His axe was heavy from hacking and hewing tentacles, his legs cramped and sore from running from one foe to the next. He was exhausted. It seemed he'd been fighting for years, though it was, perhaps, several hours.

Another of the foul tentacled beasts leapt at his head. He was too tired to move away. Laguz, the dwarfen rune of imagination and psychic matters, blazed on the head of his axe. The creature landed on a barrier of invisible force inches from his head. Gurken pulled the creature off with one hand, set it on the ground, and crushed it under heel.

Gimnur Hammerfist - the dwarven babysitter sent by the temple of Durstin to watch over the trio only to be killed by giant ants - walked up to Gurken.

"The dwarves have had it," he said. "We've had a better time of it since the goblins joined, but there are too many of these beasts and too few of us left. If only..." Gimnur trailed off.

Gurken nodded. "If only I'd been here sooner."

Twenty more tentacled things charged and were intercepted by goblins. The goblins stabbed with spears, killing several before the rest latched onto their heads. The goblins under the control of the creatures attacked the goblins not under their control. Ten goblins under control of the creatures came away from the skirmish. Two dwarves ran over

THE BERSERKER AND THE PEDANT

and hacked at them. The goblins died quickly, but not before one of the dwarves was killed by an errant goblin spear.

"Twenty tentacles become eighteen controlled goblins," Gimnur said. "Eighteen controlled goblins become ten controlled goblins after fighting other goblins. Ten controlled goblins manage to kill one dwarf. You've got to hand it to those elves, that's quite the efficient plan. Before you arrived, twenty of those foul creatures were killing thirty good dwarves."

"The lives of fifty goblins traded for that of thirty dwarves," Gurken said. "I've never had a head for math, but it seems to me that fifty is more than thirty."

"They're goblins, Gurken. They live but five years. Dwarves live two hundred. That's six thousand years of dwarven life traded for two hundred years of goblin."

Gurken looked at Gimnur with disgust. "You've learned math from the elves."

"You mean, I've learned to multiply? I've known how for some time."

Gurken shook his head sadly. "Your head may know how to multiply, Gimnur, but your heart has forgotten how to count. Don't discount the life of a goblin, don't devalue their contribution. We do battle this way because we must. We trade the lives of less effective warriors for the lives of more effective warriors, but that does not mean the cost is less."

They looked back and saw what was left of their army. A thousand... now nine hundred and ninety-nine goblins and fifty ragged, tired dwarves.

A familiar voice came from behind. "Surrender, Gurken. This world is ours!"

They turned to see Arthur, orbs gleaming in the air about his head, tentacled creatures spreading out behind him as far as they could see. Three Pellonias stepped out from behind him.

"They got you, Arthur?" Gurken asked, frowning. "What have you done to Pellonia?"

"I'm with the Phage, and the Pellonias are with me, Gurken. Soon, you'll be with us, too, or you'll be dead." All four orbs unleashed their full power towards Gurken. Flames rippled, ice cracked and lightning crackled, a beam of light pierced the air. Dwarfen runes glowed on Gurken's axe and the powers of the orbs struck an invisible shield in front of Gurken. Gurken stood there, unmoving. His lip curled.

"It will take more than Leon's toys to get to me, Arthur."

"Fortunately, we came prepared," Arthur said. He waved an arm forward and the creatures swarmed towards them. The goblins ran toward the writhing swarm and Gurken marveled at their courage. The tentacles made short work of the goblins, devouring their minds even as they made contact. The dwarves came up on either side of Gimnur and Gurken, and stood ready to receive the charge.

As the goblins and tentacled creatures swarmed down the valley, there was a loud TOCH TOCH TOCH and an enormous trench collapsed under the goblins and many of the tentacles, who fell to their deaths. Ants of various sizes streamed out of the newly formed gorge, devouring tentacles as they came. A tentacle latched onto the head of an enormous ant and was swarmed by smaller ants, which ripped it to shreds with strong pincers.

The tentacles latched onto smaller ants and squeezed, crushing them, but were themselves overrun by more ants.

Gurken got out his sleep sack and stepped inside of it, pulling it over his head. Gimnur watched Gurken for a moment, then did the same with his sleep sack. The other dwarves, not understanding what their leader was doing, nevertheless took out their own sleep sacks and piled inside. Giant ants grabbed the sacks and climbed into the gorge.

An ant the size of a kitten approached Arthur amidst the chaos. The ant stood ten feet from Arthur and looked up at him, antennae quivering. The Pellonias patted their legs and gestured for Antic to come closer. Antic sniffed the air, but didn't approach. He flexed his pincers at Arthur.

"Well, well, Antic," Arthur said, ignoring the Pellonias. His brow furled. "Nicely played. It seems we have a nemesis we didn't consider. We may not take this world through overwhelming force, but one way or the other, we will take it."

Antic spit a gooey substance at Arthur, then turned and skittered back down the gorge. Arthur stepped to the side as an enormous ant burrowed up from underground. Flames shot out of Arthur's orb; the giant ant crackled and shriveled in the heat. Arthur set his orbs to burning, freezing, beaming, and shocking a path through the battle and walked back toward the alien ship, the Pellonias following behind.

Epilogue

Arthur walked into the hall of wizards, dressed in his silken wizarding robes and carrying an oaken staff. On the tip of the staff sat the orb of light. The tap-tap of the staff striking the floor echoed through the hall as he strode down a long red carpet with mystic symbols embroidered along the edges. Wizards of the lower ranks sat near the entrance. As Arthur walked down the hall toward the eight seats of power on the far side, the rank, importance, and power of the wizards on either side of him grew.

Arthur strode up to the eight seats of power, the epicenter of mystical might in this world. The most powerful wizards sat before him, and those powerful enough to scheme to take their place flanked him. He was surrounded by the strongest wizards the world had to offer.

Arthur stood before them, holding the gaze of the wizard at the center of it all, the acknowledged leader of the wizards and the greatest living mystical talent. The throne behind her rose high, in almost comical proportions. She wore black silken wizarding robes and a matching hat with twisting black silken horns.

"Well, Arthur," she said. "You've petitioned to speak before the assembled body of the wizarding council. Please, speak your mind."

Arthur nodded. "First, a small matter. I wish it enshrined before this body that the correct possessive form of the word dwarf is dwarven, not dwarfen."

A murmur spread throughout the hall.

"You wish to spend this august body's time on triviality when this world is being invaded?" she said. "I thought you had matters of import, matters that would change the way we viewed the world. Why else would we allow you, a wizard of the tenth rank, to address us?"

"Grammar is no small matter, grand wizard. It's the basis of the control of magic. Properly phrased spells are of the highest import, for when wielding the powers of magic, a misused term could result in catastrophe! The meaning of words also gives power to an idea, and it's important that this distinction be drawn so that those who are our enemies don't have power drawn to them."

A grumbling of acknowledgement and agreement filtered through the room.

"Very well," said the high wizard, dismissively. "All in favor of using dwarven as the possessive instead of dwarfen?"

The cry of "aye" echoed through the halls.

"All against?"

Silence.

"There you have it, Arthur. Please, continue. And come to the point quick."

THE BERSERKER AND THE PEDANT

Arthur nodded.

"A follow-up. It's always rankled me that the word 'it' shouldn't have an apostrophe when used possessively, as nearly all other pronouns do. Why should that be 'the grand wizard's seat' and 'its seat' instead of 'it's seat'?"

"Outrageous!" came a cry from some wizard in the audience. A murmur, louder than the first, reverberated through the hall.

"I propose we flip the usage of an apostrophe in its, so that it's is possessive and its is the contractive."

The council of wizards burst into an uproar.

"Scandalous!" someone yelled.

"Heathen!" yelled another.

"Get him out of here!"

"Disaster!" the shouts continued.

The grand wizard stood and raised an arm; silence fell through the hall. She shook her head. "Arthur, you've wasted our time. It's not going to happen. I won't even bring such blasphemy to a vote."

"Oh, its going to happen," Arthur said. Three orbs sprung from under his wizarding robes, and fire, ice and lighting rained upon the seats of power. The strongest wizards in the realm threw their arms up reflexively, working together to form a powerful barrier, staving back the aggressive blasts.

"Intentoque lux trabem!" Arthur said, sounding

bored.

The light in the room dimmed. Several wizards instinctually called to their orbs and staves for light, but the light flowed towards the orb like smoke to a sucking fan. A powerful stream of blindingly white light poured forth from the orb on top of Arthur's staff and pierced the defensive magics of the most powerful wizards of the wizarding council, slicing through them in half a moment. The back of the tall throne fell with a tremendous crash. It was over before anyone else could react and light returned to the room.

Tap-tap. Arthur's staff, the tip glowing with the radiance of the sun, echoed through the silence of the great hall as he walked to the large throne in the center, pushed the former grand wizard's corpse off the seat and sat down. He leaned over and pulled off her wizarding hat, placing it upon his head.

"If anyone else is against changing it's to its, please speak now."

"I-" a wizard managed to get out before a white-hot laser burned a hole in his head.

No one else spoke.

Arthur glared around the room. "Very well, then let us vote. All those in favor?"

Silence.

Arthur burned a hole through the head of another wizard.

"Aye." The low murmur echoed around the

room.

"Then its so, it's shall henceforth be its and its, it's. Now that that unpleasantness is over, its time to get down to business..." Arthur tapped his staff down in three loud, stiff strikes against the floor.

A hundred tentacled creatures, the last remnants of the invading Phage, dropped from the high ceilings, ensnaring wizards of every rank. There were more wizards than creatures and some of the creatures died before they could control their prey, but most struck their mark. The most powerful wizards of the wizarding council were now under Phage control.

Harold absentmindedly reached into the bag of potato chips while watching the computer monitor. His fingers closed on nothing. He looked in the bag. There was nothing but crumbs. He sighed.

"Well, there goes the best part of the day," Harold said. He turned the bag upside down, emptying the crumbs into his mouth and licking the oil off his fingers.

A red flashing light appeared on the monitor. Harold took a swig of his soda, emptying the can. He tried to crush it with his hand, but it only dented a little. He threw it towards the recycling bin, but it bounced off the rim and fell to the ground. He scrunched his lips to one side and wiped the last of the oil off his hands and onto his shirt.

"Well, let's see what this alert's all about," Harold said. He grabbed the mouse and moved the cursor over the flashing light and double-clicked it. That brought up Bugzilla, the bug tracking software they also used to track important requests. They hadn't brought anything on board specifically to track important requests, and apparently no one wanted to spend their Awakening working on something as trivial as ticket tracking software, so Bugzilla it was. The alert was a priority one bug.

"Oh-ho, a P1," said Harold. "This might be an interesting day after all."

He opened the bug and read the title.

It read, "Two subjects requesting immediate transportation off planet M4D-058." Harold clicked the link to look at the description. It read, "Melanie Amadi and Penelope Amadi for immediate evacuation from planet M4D-058. Click here to execute transport."

Harold smiled, remembering a bag of mixed nuts and chocolate he'd saved. He opened the drawer on the side of his desk and dug around for it. He found it and tore it open. He poured some into one hand and tossed them in his mouth, one piece at a time. He clicked on the execute transport link and spun his chair around to face the transport pad.

Two transparent tubes large enough to hold a person lit up a bright yellow from the LEDs that formed a ring inside. A monofilament cable unspooled from the tubes beneath the ship, guided by artificial gravity and nanobot workers, descending toward the planet's surface. After a few moments, the spools stopped spinning with a metallic ker-chunk. They spooled back so fast, it made a whizzing sound.

Harold stood up, cleaning his hands on his pants, and wiped the crumbs off his clothing. Two figures zipped up the tubes. Melanie stepped out a large hole in the front of the tube, the monofilament cable releasing her automatically. Penelope stood in the tube, mouth open, eyes comically wide, looking around the room.

"Did you see it?" Melanie asked. "Where'd it go?"

"Where'd what go?" Harold asked.

"It. The Phage. It had ahold of me, now it's gone."

Harold shrugged. "I didn't see anything," he said. "You can always report to the decontamination chamber." Harold pointed to a door. On the door was a sign that read "Showers."

Melanie spun around, looking around the room. "I guess it fell off," she said. She shuddered. "I think I will take a shower." She turned to Penelope, saying, "Wait here; I'll come back and get you in a few minutes and we'll get you situated." Melanie ran to the shower room.

Harold looked at Penelope. She appeared to be a

girl of twelve, but Harold knew that didn't mean anything. She could be a thousand years old; she had the gift that prevented her from aging. She was the All-Mother's granddaughter, after all, and the All-Mother decided which humans were worthy of the gift. Harold always did the prudent thing, and when your bosses' bosses' grand-daughter appeared, that meant keeping quiet and keeping your head down.

Penelope didn't seem to agree. "Pardon me," Penelope said. "But is there any way you can get me out of this thing?"

Harold pointed towards himself, eyes raised in a questioning look.

"Yes, you," Penelope said. "There's nobody else here!"

Harold crinkled his brow. "You just step out, Penelope, the cord will let go."

Penelope stepped out of the tube, and the monofilament cord released her.

"Thanks," Penelope said. "But my name's Pellonia."

Harold shook his head. "Nah, that was your name on M4D-058, your 'fantasy name,' if you will.'" Harold did air quotes with his fingers. "Your real name's Penelope."

"Oh," Penelope said. She stood there for a minute, then said, "What's your name?"

"I'm Harold Douglas, System Support

THE BERSERKER AND THE PEDANT

Administrator slash Analyst slash Engineer. Seventh grade."

She nodded toward his desk. "What's that?"

Harold looked at his desk. "You mean my desk?"

"No, not your desk." Pellonia crossed her arms. "The rectangular image on top of it."

"You really haven't been on the ship before, have you?"

"Nope."

"That's called a screen; it's part of the computer."

"Oh, of course. Makes sense. Yup. What's a computer?"

"Wow, you've got a lot to learn. Leon's gonna have fun with you. He loves to torment greenies, and given how he died on M4D-058, he's not especially happy with you."

"You heard about that, eh?"

"Oh, everyone's heard about that. It's all over the ship. I think it's all over the galaxy - well, at least everyone in this system knows about it."

Penelope scratched her head, frowning. "Can you use the screen to help my friends?"

"Sorry, we can't help anyone on planet. The ship left orbit as soon as you and Melanie got on board. No one wants to wait around here and see how things play out with the Phage. Your friends are on their own."

"But we'll be back in five years, right?" Penelope asked.

"Do you mean five years planetside? I doubt it, Penelope. The battle didn't exactly kick off well. All-Mother will probably just abandon the planet an-"

Penelope crinkled her brow. "My name is Pellonia. I don't care what this All-Mother thinks. We will come back."

Harold smiled. "Heh. If you say so, space elf. Welcome to the Awakening."

Afterword

If you enjoyed *The Berserker and the Pedant*, please review it!

Join my mailing list and I'll send you a free short story detailing Arthur's resurrections from Harold's point of view. It's a hilarious insight into the world of the elves on board their ship and it's not available anywhere else.

The next book in the series, *Dragon Apocalypse*, is available for pre-order on Amazon and work is underway for a graphic novel adaptation, the first sketches have already arrived. The crowdfunding campaign is about to begin, so if you want early access and to watch a graphic novel come to life, please check it out on Kickstarter.

If you'd like keep updated as I publish new stories, send an email to josh@pedantpublishing.com and I'll add you to my email list or find me on twitter @seasoup. The most difficult part of being a writer is getting discovered by your audience. Please leave a review and recommend the book to your friends, that's the best way for people to discover my writing.

Let me know if you leave a review and I'll send you a copy of *Dragon Apocalypse* for free when it comes out.

You can keep up with my stories at http://www.pedantpublishing.com.

Thank you for reading, and I hope to see you again soon!

    The Berserker and the Pedant

        available on
        Goodreads
        Amazon
        Audible

About the Author

JOSH POWELL, wielder of the Sommerswerd, destroyer of the thread, expeditioner to Barrier Peaks, discoverer of his magic talent, and venturer into the Tomb of Horrors is known for having survived a harrowing adolescence full of danger and fantasy. He's gone on to write *The Berserker and the Pedant*. He is frantically scribbling away at the sequel, *Dragon Apocalypse* and working on several other novels, *Vagabond Necromancer*, *Space Elf*, and *Primacy: Exile*.

He also spends some not inconsiderable amount of time wiggling his fingers over a keyboard as a software engineer. He lives with his wife, Marianne, and two amazing children, Liam and Chloe, in sunny California, where winter is, most decidedly, never coming.

by Josh Powell

The Berserker and the Pedant

eBook

Audio

Graphic Novel

Dragon Apocalypse

Available on Pre-order Now!

You may also enjoy books by Joel Babbitt

Camallay: An Infinite Worlds Novel (Marik's Marauders)

eBook

Paladin of a Hidden God (Series)

The Trials of Caste

Into the Heart of Evil

The Game of Fates

Made in the USA
Columbia, SC
15 March 2021